GW01045084

IN THE ARMS OF A

Savage

III

K.L. HALL

IN THE ARMS OF A
Savage
III

K.L. HALL

All characters appearing in this work are fictitious. Any resemblance to real persons, living or dead, is purely coincidental. In the Arms of a Savage 3. Copyright © 2017 K. L. Hall. All rights reserved. No part of this book may be used or reproduced in any manner whatsoever without written permission except in the case of brief quotations embodied in critical articles or reviews.

Dedication

To all the aspiring authors out there.

The journey may be long, but don't stop doing what you love to do. Remember, Rome wasn't built in a day, so don't lose your desire to hustle. You'll make it to the top when it's your time.

Acknowledgments

Always first, I would like to give thanks to my Lord and Savior, Jesus Christ. Without him, nothing I do would be possible. To my family, friends, and James, thank you for your continuous support, encouragement, and love. To my pen sisters and brothers, I thank you all for your support and empowerment. Lastly, to my readers, old and new alike, I thank you so much for taking the time to read, review, and spread the word about the *In the Arms of a Savage* series.

-K.L. Hall

Synopsis

They say friends make the worst enemies, but what about family? The Calloway and Price family secret was supposed to be taken to the grave. Now that Raquel knows the connection between the feuding families and the man she loves is presumed dead, she must figure out her next move. Will she succumb to the fast and dangerous life of the streets to avenge the man she loves, or will the one skeleton from her past spill the secret that unravels everything?

Everyone thinks dead men tell no tales, but not when it comes to Law Calloway. Now that the people he loves and those who hate him the most think he's dead, he's free to make his moves in silence and lay out his plan on his quest to gain the ultimate respect—starting with getting the Feds and the Price family off his back once and for all.

In the finale of this ride-or-die love story, everyone is seeking their revenge by *any* means necessary. When secrets come pouring out like rain, will real love be enough to conquer all? For all parties involved, it's not the beginning of the story that concerns them. It's not knowing how it will all end.

Epigraph

"Her attitude is savage, but her heart is pure gold."

CHAPTER ONE

Raquel

My heart stopped.

It ached. It bled. It broke repeatedly like a broken record or a nightmare I couldn't wake up from. The longer I stared at him, the more my eyes burned. The only thing I could think to do was open my mouth and let out the loudest scream my lungs and vocal chords would allow. The second I took my eyes off Law, I turned to see Blaze shooting back at Dallas and his brother. Camille and Nevaeh were on their knees screaming, and the preacher was laid out behind us with a pool of blood underneath him. His crimson blood seeped onto my dress as I laid there with Law. It was all one big mess. I couldn't tell whose blood was whose. I didn't even know if the preacher was still breathing or not. I could barely tell if I was breathing, or if it was all one big, bad dream.

There were bullet holes in the wooden pews and a few of the stained-glass windows were shattered. My small bouquet was lying on the ground with specks of blood on the flowers. I closed my eyes as a tear slipped out. This wasn't how my wedding was supposed to go. I was supposed to have married the man I loved, but instead, he was lying next to me dead.

"Baby! Baby! Please, don't do this! Please, wake up! Law! No! You can't leave me!" I yelled.

I held the sides of his face and looked for any sign of life in his body, but I couldn't see a thing. My eyes were glazed over with tears, and my vision was blurry. I could feel the mascara and eyeliner running down my face and staining my cheeks.

"Please, Law. No! I love you! Please, come back to me!" I sobbed as I laid my cheek against his forehead.

His body was still warm, which comforted me if only for the moment. When the gunshots stopped, everything went dead silent. I looked up at everybody, and they all were looking back at me. I could read the looks on all their faces. Blaze's was filled with anger. His nostrils flared like an angry dragon, but his eyes were glossy. I knew the moment he blinked, tears would fall out. Nevaeh's hand was on her stomach as tears flew from her eyes. She scurried to her feet and ran over to Blaze. Law's mother sat still, clutching her chest and staring at her son lying beside me. Lastly, I looked over at Camille. She was crouched down between two church pews with both of her hands clasped together over her head as if she was in the middle of a tornado drill. I could tell her heart broke for me. The sorrowful looks were almost too much to bear.

"Raquel..." she said as she slowly stood to her feet.

I threw my hand up to cut her off.

"No. Don't... Please, don't say anything," I said barely above a whisper.

I looked back at Law. Time was frozen as I stared at him. I didn't know how I was even going to stand up. I felt like I was destined to live in the nightmare that my life had turned into from the moment I stepped off the plane in Miami. Only now, I was destined to live with the heartache of losing Law.

"We need to call the police," Nevaeh said, breaking the silence.

We all stared at her and shook our heads.

"We can't do that," his mother said.

"What? Are you serious? Why not! There's been a murder here! In a church! The police are going to be all over this! If we don't call it in, it'll look like we had something to do with it!"

"C'mon, Nevaeh. Let me take you home," Blaze told her.

"What? What is wrong with all of you? So, nobody is going to call 911? What are you scared of? Huh? You know what? Fine. I'll do it!" she said.

Nevaeh pulled out her cell phone and held it in her shaky hands. She unlocked the phone and tried to dial 911. Blaze quickly reached over and snatched her phone away.

"Let me get you out of here, okay? I'll take you home, and I'll come back and clean all this up," he said, dragging her out of the church.

"Blaze, what the fuck is going on here?" I heard her yell before the doors slammed.

I knew Nevaeh was going to have more questions, and I was glad I didn't have to be in the car with her when she asked them. As much as I wanted to call the police, I knew telling them that Law Calloway had been murdered wouldn't do anything but shed unnecessary light on all of us. The truth was, we all needed to stay as far away from the police as possible whether we liked it or not. I shook my head and threw up my hands. Nothing was going to get accomplished with the three of us standing there. No resolution was going to come out of the fucked up situation we were in. We were all praying for a miracle with empty hearts. I slowly climbed to my feet and walked over to the second pew to grab a suit jacket that someone had left. I gently laid it over Law's face as I wiped my eyes with the back of my hand.

"Take me home," I told Camille.

* * *

3

Blaze

It seemed like as soon as Nevaeh got in the car, questions started rolling off her tongue about why no one wanted to call the police, why everyone looked so calm, and what the fuck was really going on with my family.

"What don't I know?" she asked as she tightly folded her arms across her chest.

"What are you talkin' about?"

"What the fuck do you mean what am I talking about? I just saw your fucking brother get murdered in cold fucking blood on his wedding day! His fucking wedding day! What the fuck is going on, Blaze? You need to tell me the truth right now. I'm not leaving this car until you do!"

I blew hot air out of my mouth as I shook my head. Her ass wasn't going to quit until I gave her some type of information. I didn't know how green she was until that moment. I figured that since I met her in the strip club, she would have known a thing or two about how hood niggas got down, but I was wrong. The only thing that kept replaying in my mind every time she asked something new was the fact that when we first met, she told me that she wanted to go to school to be a lawyer. That didn't say shit to me but that we operated on two opposite sides of the law. For that fact alone, I knew I couldn't tell her too much, even if she was about to be my baby mama.

"Look, I'm sorry you had to witness any of that shit, okay? But shit is more complicated than it seems. I don't even know how to put it into words that you'll understand."

"Try me," she said, softening her look.

"I know the niggas that did that shit."

"Don't you think that's even more reason to go to the police?" she asked.

"In a perfect world, maybe. But not in my family, aight? We don't run around lookin' for the police. They usually come lookin' for us."

"So, you're sayin' all this to say what?"

"I'm sayin'... ain't nothin' the police gon' do for me and mine but get in the mix of shit and fuck it up more than it already is. I gotta handle this on my own."

"Wait. Handle what exactly? The niggas that came into your brother's wedding with guns blazing? Nigga, are you dumb or stupid? They just murdered your brother! Your flesh and blood! What makes you think they won't do the same to you with no questions asked?"

I clenched my teeth and listened to them grind against one another. I really wanted her to drop the whole thing, but I knew better. Hearing her say the words that my brother, my flesh and fuckin' blood was gone, was driving me insane. My adrenaline was still pumping on 1,000, so I hadn't had the time to process what I'd just witnessed. I could remember a time when I was younger where all I had was Law. Wolfe was too grown to wanna deal with me. Law saved my life when we were just kids, and although I wasn't a kid anymore, he was still saving my ass up until the moment those Price niggas took him from me.

"Blaze, did you hear me?" she asked, interrupting my thoughts.

"Can you just drop the shit, Heaven?"

"Drop it? No! Blaze, in case you forgot, your baby is growing inside me day by day! Do you wanna be around to meet your child, or do you plan on running out and getting yourself killed before it's even born? Just let me know now!"

"Heaven, just shut the fuck up, aight? Goddamn!" I yelled as I smacked the steering wheel.

I let the baritone in my voice ring out to shut her up. I couldn't stand to even hear her talk anymore. All I wanted her to do was get the fuck out of my car so I could go handle my business.

"You're tellin' me to shut the fuck up, really? Really, Blaze?" she said, smacking her lips together.

"I just lost my mothafuckin' brother back there, and all this extra shit you talkin' ain't makin' shit better for either one of us. So yes, Heaven, shut the fuck up and let me process this shit!" I yelled.

Heaven flopped back in the passenger seat and turned her head out of the window. We rode in silence until I heard her sniffling with her back to me. As annoyed as I was with her, I still wanted to know what her problem was. I sighed and licked my lips before I spoke, knowing I was probably going to regret it.

"Heaven..."

She shook her head and wiped her face.

"I know you hear me callin' your name, girl. Look at me," I told her.

"What?"

"Why you cryin', huh? What's wrong with you?"

"I don't know," she said, shaking her head. "I—I feel bad for coming at you like that. Like, you're right. You just lost your brother. I don't know what I'd do if I lost my sister, especially the way you did. I don't know. I feel like a bitch for being so insensitive, but at the same time, I give a fuck about you, Blaze. More importantly, I give a fuck about this baby, our baby. I want you to be here. I don't want to go through this shit alone. I'm just scared."

She wiped her face with both hands. I pulled up to the front of her apartment complex and put my car in park before I turned to look at her.

"I get it," I told her as I reached out to wipe her tears with my thumb. "Don't worry about me, Heaven. I'm going to be just fine."

"Yeah. I'm sure Law told Raquel the same thing, and look at what happened to him. Now, her whole world is ruined, and she's alone," she said.

I nodded as I processed her comment. She was right. I was sure he told Raquel all the same bullshit that I was telling Heaven just to keep the peace and keep a smile on her face the best way he knew how. Truth was, with the last name Calloway, we were born with a target on our back. I walked around every day not knowing when I was going to take my last breath because a nigga felt like taking my life. I never knew if I was going to be okay, fine, or any of that shit, but it sounded good.

"Look, I gotta get back to my family. Are you gonna be okay?"

"I'll be fine."

"Okay." I nodded.

"Promise me you'll call me when you get the chance. Please?"

"I will."

Heaven unhooked her seatbelt and reached over to hug me. I put the car in park and wrapped my arms around her waist. The sweet smell of her perfume made me stop and close my eyes for a second to just enjoy the moment. I knew when I left her, I'd be forced to deal with the reality of living in a world without my brother by my side. That was a world I wasn't ready to face. I gave her waist a tight squeeze and then tried to pull away. Her body was shaking, and I could tell she didn't want to let me go.

"C'mon, Heaven. I gotta go. I'll call you when I can, aight?"

She nodded her head against my shoulder and turned to get out of the car. I watched her walk into her building. Once she was safely inside, I put the car in drive and headed back to the church to tend to my brother.

* * *

Law

As soon as Blaze, Nevaeh, Raquel, and Camille left the church, I opened my eyes to see my mother still sitting there.

"You can get up, Law. They're gone now," she told me.

My mother walked over and helped me sit up slowly. I felt like I'd been repeatedly hit in the chest with a baseball bat. Although my chest stung like a bitch, the vest had eaten up the bullets that were supposed to have killed me. My mother slid the bloody suit jacket off my arms as I unbuttoned my shirt and took it off so that I could open the vest. My chest was red and sore, but I was still breathing.

"You need to hurry up and get out of here. Your brother is probably on his way back here now to help me clean up this mess," she said, looking down at the preacher.

"Okay." I nodded as I struggled to stand to my feet.

I held my chest with one hand while picking up my jacket with the other. I glanced over at my mother who was shaking her head at me with tears in her eyes.

"Are you sure you know what you're doing, Law?" she asked.

"I do."

She sighed as she walked over to me.

"I don't have a good feeling about this."

"Hey. They wanted a battle, so I'm giving them niggas a war. I know what I'm doing, Ma. I promise. Thank you for helping me pull this off," I told her.

My mother nodded and wrapped her arms around me. I knew she was the only person I could trust with my plan. She would never tell on me, and she damn sure would never go to the police. After the two of us had a talk about why she told Blaze about her cancer and not me, we came to an understanding, and I let her in on my plan just a week before I did it.

"Ma," I called out as I walked into the guest house.

"I'm back in the room. Give me a second," she told me.

I nodded and walked into the living room to sit down. Cigarette ash covered the coffee table, and the TV was turned up way too loud.

"I didn't know you started smoking again," I said to her as soon as she came out to join me.

"I picked up the habit when I was fifteen. I kicked it by the time I was twenty-one. This right here is recreational smoking."

"Recreational?"

"Yeah. I do it every now and then. You know? For pleasure."

"Oh." I shrugged.

As much as I wanted to give her shit for smoking knowing she was sick, I knew everything I was going to say was going to go in one ear and out the other. My mother had never let me or anyone else tell her what to do, and I was sure she wasn't about to start then. So, instead of pressing the issue, I changed the subject.

"How are you feeling?" I asked.

"I'm okay. The doctor just left not too long ago. I just took my medicine."

"What'd he say?"

"Nothing has changed, Andreas," she told me as she walked over and dumped a cup of water into her large house plant.

I slowly shook my head, wishing for better news.

9

"So, did you come here to feel sorry for your mother, or did you come here to talk?" she asked.

"I came to talk."

"What's on your mind, Andreas? I can tell you've been stressing."

"How you know that?"

"Haven't I always told y'all I know you all better than you know yourselves, huh? That hasn't changed."

I curved my lips into a half smile and nodded.

"Well, yeah. I've been a little stressed."

"About what?"

"Just trying to make my next move my best move. You know what I mean? I just feel like I got too many eyes on me right now, and I can't move how I want to. I just know if I don't put an end to this Price and Calloway shit, a nigga ain't never gon' sleep sound again. I'm always gon' be lookin' over my shoulder, trying to figure out if today is gon' be my last day. That ain't no way to live."

"So, what are you thinking about doing?" she asked.

"I need to make my moves in silence. I'm setting some shit up, and I don't want nobody in on it, so that's why I'm coming to you."

"What do you need me to do, Andreas?"

I looked down at my shoes and then back up to make eye contact with her.

"I need you to help me fake my death..."

My mother promised me that she would take care of everything so that I could do the things I needed to do, and I trusted her word. She'd never lied to me before. Outside of Raquel, she was the only other woman to truly have my back.

"Give me your phone," she told me. "I'll hold onto it until you need it. There's $100,000 in cash in the bag underneath the last pew along with the keys to your father's old stash house in Pembroke Pines. Take the car that's parked behind the church. The keys are underneath the driver's seat."

"Okay. Thank you," I said as I held both of her shoulders.

I rubbed my chest again, kissed her forehead, and headed to the back of the church.

"You should really get your chest looked at," she called out.

"I can't. I'm dead, remember?"

"Stop saying that!" she yelled, swatting her hands in the air.

"Wait... what about the preacher?" I asked as I looked back and his body lying in the same pool of blood as my suit jacket.

"I'll take care of it all." She nodded. "Now, hurry up before your brother gets back. And Andreas... please, be careful."

"I will," I told her, as I grabbed the bag from underneath the pew and exited the church like she'd instructed.

Now that the judge dismissed the whole case against me and my family and the Price brothers thought I was dead, I could sit back, observe, and see where the chips landed while still carrying out my plan.

* * *

Dallas

As soon as Darius and I ran out of the church, we jumped in the car and sped down the highway, heading straight to our father's house to give him the good news that we all had been waiting to happen. Law was finally dead, and it would only be a matter of time before we put a bullet in Blaze's head and ended the feud between our families once and for all. Then, there would be no question about who really ran Miami.

"Yo, I'm hype as fuck right now, D. Did you see the way that nigga's body flew back and hit the ground like that?" Darius said, boasting about the kill shot that sent Law to meet his maker.

"Hell yeah. All those fuckin' screams were like music to my mothafuckin' ears," I told him. "I'm gon' sleep like a baby tonight."

Darius and I both let out loud laughs and dapped each other up.

"Hell yeah, man. This shit feels good as a bitch. I didn't think it would ever feel this good to kill a mothafucka, but damn. This one is for you, baby!" he said, kissing his hand and raising it up to the sky to pay respect to our oldest brother, Damien.

"Hell yeah. One time for our fallen soldier, man." I nodded and looked up to the sky.

"I can't wait to hear what Dad is gon' say about this shit."

"Yo, uh... speakin' of Dad. Did he ever talk to you about Damien?"

"What about him?"

"About anything... you know... after he died." I shrugged.

"Nah, not that I can think of right now. Why? What's up? Is there somethin' I need to know?" he asked.

"Nah, it's nothin'. I was just wondering."

Darius scoffed and shook his head from left to right.

"Nigga, I already know you lyin', so you might as well go on and tell me now."

"I just came across some information not too long ago about him. That's all."

"Information? What kind of information? Stop bein' so damn elusive, nigga."

"Elusive? Nigga, since when you start using words like *elusive* and shit?" I asked, frowning my forehead at him.

"What's wrong with a nigga expanding his vocabulary, huh?

But nah, I been strokin' this new bitch for a little minute now. She a school teacher and shit."

"A school teacher, nigga? Really?"

He flashed me an unapologetic smile and nodded.

"Yeah. That bitch be teachin' me all types of words when I be hittin' her pussy from the back. She just be yellin' out mad crazy shit like psychomancy and hypogeal. That shit is wild." He laughed.

"Nigga, what the fuck does any of that shit even mean?"

"I don't know, but when she be moanin' that shit sound sexy as hell."

I burst out laughing and shook my head at him.

"Yo, nigga, you a stone-cold fool for that shit."

"Hey, ain't nothin' wrong with expanding your mind. You know a nigga ain't go to college, so this is free higher learning right here. That's just how I look at it."

"Yeah, aight."

"But nah, back to Damien. What about him? What type of information did you get?"

I took a quick glance at him and then focused my attention back on the road.

"What if I told you that he wasn't our full-blooded brother but more like half?"

"Hold the fuck up. What? What do you mean he wasn't our full-blooded brother? He looked just like Pops did when he was comin' up in the game," he said.

"Look, Pops had him with another bitch before he had us with Mom, aight?"

"And how the fuck do you even know any of this shit? Huh? Pops told you or somethin'?"

"Nah. Somebody else told me, but I'm still lookin' into the shit, so don't say shit to Pops about it until I know more, aight?"

"Okay, but who was this other bitch who Pops supposedly had Damien with?"

"I don't think you'd believe me if I told you, nigga."

13

"Who was it?"

"Law and Blaze's mother."

"What the fuck!"

"Yeah, exactly."

"And you really believe the mothafucka who told you all this shit? It sounds like a bunch of bullshit if you ask me."

"I don't know right now. That's why I'm tellin' your ass to sit on this fuckin' information and keep a tight lip until I know more, aight?"

"Aight, say no more," he said, throwing both hands up in the air. "You gon' go see Shiya tonight and give her ass the news too?"

"I don't know. I might." I shrugged.

"How you think she gon' react?"

"I don't know. I guess she'll be happy. This is what she wanted."

"It's what we all wanted." He nodded.

"Yeah, you right."

"What's up with you?"

"Me? What do you mean?" I asked.

"I don't know. It just seems like you would've been happier than you are to get rid of the nigga that stole your girl."

"He ain't steal shit from me. Get that shit straight, nigga. If I wanted her, I would've kept her. Even when she was with that nigga, you saw who she kept runnin' back to, right?"

"You know what I mean, nigga. Damn. I'm just sayin'. I feel you though. You got the juice, nigga." He chuckled.

"Shut up. I'm straight," I said as I pulled into our father's driveway and shut the engine off. "Remember what I told you about that Damien shit, nigga."

"Don't worry, nigga. I got it. I won't say shit."

We both got out of the car and walked around the back of our father's house in Palmetto Bay. Darius knocked on the door while I stood back and rested my hands on top of my head. When our father made his way to open his home to us, he looked us up and down.

"You're both here to tell me good news I hope," he said.

"Yeah, we are." Darius nodded.

"Come in then."

I followed Darius into our father's study and took my seat across the room from him. He was moving slower than usual, even with his walking cane.

"How's your knee doing, Pop?" I asked.

"It's a little stiff today. That's why I got this goddamn cane. I feel like I'm seventy-two or something," he said, shaking his head.

"How often did the doctor tell you to use it?"

"Only when I need it. I can usually get around fine without it, but I could barely get out of the damn bed this morning."

My father sat down and rubbed his hand over his knee. I still remember years ago when I got the call from Damien that our father had been shot. I immediately assumed the worse, but I was happy to see that he'd only been shot in his knee. Although it had been completely shattered, the surgeons were able to reconstruct it. For the most part, he was self-sufficient, but there were days where he experienced pain and would get frustrated when he couldn't move around like he once used to.

"But enough about me. Is the job done?" he asked.

"It's done.," I nodded.

My father nodded slowly as he tapped his cane against the ground.

"Now that's what the fuck I like to hear!"

"So, what's next?" Darius asked. "There's still one more, the youngest one, Blaze."

"He'll be the easiest to kill unlike the other two now that he's all alone with nobody to protect him. I trust that you can make that happen, Dallas? After all, you are the oldest in charge now."

"I know what to do," I told him.

"Good. I'll help set you up, and then you'll take it down," he told me.

"As always." I nodded.

"Did you see the look on anybody's faces when you two

busted into the wedding? I bet their fuckin' mother was as pale as a ghost!" he said, barreling out a loud chuckle.

I watched him reach over and grab his cigarette box, pull one out, and then light it. He adjusted himself in his chair so that he could access the ashtray and then shook with more laugher.

"Hell yeah. None of they asses saw that shit coming at all," Darius boasted.

"Yo, Darius. Can you give me and Pops a second?" I interrupted them.

"Uh, yeah. That's cool. I'm going to go smoke. Pops, can I get a cigarette up off you?" he asked as he walked over to the table.

"Knock yourself out, but next time, buy your own goddamn cigarettes," he said as he handed him one.

"I got you," he said, as he pulled his lighter out of his back pocket and walked outside.

I waited until he closed the door behind him, and then I turned back to address my father about the news Raquel had dropped on me.

"What made you bring her up?" I asked.

"Who?"

"They mother, that's who."

"No reason, really. I know their father is dead, so I was hoping their mother came out of hiding after all these years. I wanted her to feel the pain of losing another son first hand."

"Aight," I said as I looked at my father out of the corner of my eye.

He'd never once mentioned Law's mother before. It seemed odd to me that he would bring her name up out of the blue like that. The way he quickly tried to brush my observance off so quickly made me look at his ass funny, too. My father had always kept it a buck with the three of us ever since we were younger. He told us the who, what, when, where, why, and how of everything having to do with the streets, money, bitches, and drugs. I didn't understand why he was so quick to try and change up. It was almost as if he was too scared or nervous to talk about her out of fear of slippin' up and putting me on to some real shit. One thing was becoming clear to me- My brothers, myself, and those Calloway niggas were all just pawns in our parents fucked up love triangle. Whatever it was between us and them, I was going to get to the bottom of that shit, whether my father was going to tell me the truth or not.

CHAPTER TWO

Raquel

I spent the first night in my bed alone, laying in the bloodstained dress I'd worn to what was supposed to be my wedding just hours earlier. I couldn't shift my gaze away from Law's side of the bed. The pillow and the sheets still smelled like him. I pulled them close to me and dove my nose into them to inhale his scent. I wanted to be wrapped in it like a warm blanket. The memories of what was supposed to be my wedding day kept hanging like old pictures on a wall inside my head. I couldn't deal with the real in my reality. I curled up on the bed in the dark and cried so hard that the room started to spin as if I were intoxicated. I stopped breathing. I just cried so hard that no sound came out of my mouth. All I wanted to do was hurry up and fall asleep. I had this crazy thought in the back of my head that once I woke up, things would return to normal, and Law and I would pick up where we left off. I would be standing at the altar with my hands in his, and he would be smiling, looking right at me.

There was no such luck in that. I woke up the next day in more pieces than the day before because I knew it wasn't just a bad dream. It was all real, and Law was no longer a part of my waking life. After that revelation sunk in, I hardly left my room. I only left the bed to use the bathroom and to nibble on the food that Camille would leave outside of my bedroom door.

By the third night, I didn't care if I was a walking zombie. I was grieving, and everybody knew it. I occupied my time with smoking and drinking just to fall asleep and then waking up at half past two just to do it all over again. My misery didn't need company. It needed alcohol, marijuana, and to keep the curtains closed tight for as long as I could. As much as I tried, I couldn't hide my pain. I'd never dealt with a massive loss like that before, and it was clear I didn't know how to handle the shit. It hadn't even been an entire year since Law had come into my life, but my heart bled as if we'd known each other for a lifetime, and he was the only man I'd ever loved. I missed everything about Law from the top of his head to the soles of his feet and everything in between, his deep voice and soft lips, the way he laughed at me and with me, the way he smiled at me, and the way he smelled—everything.

As much as I wanted to keep falling apart at the seams, I knew I only had two options in front of me—keep letting my feelings take over my body and run my mind or get the fuck up and start functioning like a real human being again. I chose the latter. On day four of life without Law, I walked into the bathroom and turned on the shower for the first time. And, against my better judgment, I looked at myself in the mirror. The lack of sleep and upkeep of my body had left me with plum-colored bags under my glossy eyes. I splashed some cold water on my face and peeled off my wedding dress for the first time since the worst day of my life, my wedding day. As soon as the water hit my body, fresh tears poured out of my eyes. Although the shower water felt amazing against my skin, I just stood there, trying to stop my face from breaking into a million pieces for the millionth time.

When I stepped out, I wrapped the towel around my body and walked out of the bathroom. I jumped when I saw Camille standing beside the couch inside my room.

"Shit, Camille! You scared the shit out of me! How'd you get in here?" I asked, while clutching my chest.

It was the first time I'd spoken since I left the church. I didn't even recognize the sound of my own voice at first.

"You left the door unlocked. It's the first time I actually tried

19

to get in and see you in a few days, so I was glad it actually worked."

"Oh." I shrugged.

I pulled my towel tightly around my body and walked over to collapse face down on the couch. Camille looked at me and then moved my feet to sit beside me.

"I look like a crazy person, huh?" I asked as I turned my head to the side.

Camille quickly shook her head.

"No, you don't. You shouldn't be going through any of this shit, Raqi. My heart is just so broken for you right now, girl. Like... I don't know what to do. I be wanting to give you space then I wanna be all up underneath you so you don't have to be alone. I'm all over the place with this shit too."

I nodded and wiped my eyes. With every tear that seeped out, the more I started to unravel. I adjusted myself and laid my head on her lap as she stroked my hair. Everything was just wrong. She started rubbing my back to comfort me. As much as I wanted her to stop, I couldn't do anything but cry. I knew she was my best friend, but I was still embarrassed to be crying to her about my problems. But at the same time, I couldn't stop if I wanted to.

"I'm sorry," I told her.

"For what?"

"For my depressed ass, woe-is-me mood. I know I haven't been easy to deal with."

"Do you wanna talk about it? Or anything?"

"I don't know where to begin."

"Start with just telling me how you're feeling in this very moment."

"What is this? A ghetto ass therapy session?"

"Hell yeah. Plus, a good ol' Camille and Raquel BFF heart-to-heart chat. We're long overdue for one."

"Are we really?"

"No, but still. So, go ahead. Talk. Pour out your emotions to me. I'll be your cup."

"Please, shut up." I chuckled.

"See? It's working! You're smiling already!"

"Ugh!" I groaned. "I don't know how I feel, Camille. One minute I'm sad, like depressed as fuck, like I'm locked inside a room with no way out and no one to talk to. Then the next minute, I'm angry as hell, and I want to burn down that room and everything around it. I'm a walking fucking basket case right now. I have so much shit to figure out."

"Like what?"

"His... his funeral arrangements, if I'm going to even stay in Miami after all of this... then there's Derrick. Poor Derrick. I don't even know if he's fucking alive at this point. Yeah, what he did to me was fucked up, but he didn't deserve that shit. Then all that shit with the body and... it's just all too damn much! I can't take this shit!"

"Okay, okay. Calm down. Take a deep breath in, and blow it out through your nose. I'm going to help you figure this out from beginning to end."

"Okay." I sighed as I sat up and tried to bring my heart rate back down to a normal level.

"So, let's start with the funeral."

"I don't even know where to start. I've never done anything like this before, Camille. I've never lost anybody close to me."

"Have you talked to his mom? I mean, I know it sounds bad, but she's dealt with more death than you or I have put together."

"I don't want to bring any more pain to her doorstep. She's sick. She lost not one but three sons and a husband. I would feel like an evil person to dump all that on her."

"I get that, but you can't do it alone."

"I know." I nodded.

"What about Blaze? You think he would help?"

"I haven't seen him since everything went down at the church. I don't even know if he's in the house. It's not like I've really left the room or made the effort to try and make contact with another human being since all this shit went down."

"Yeah, I know. It's a bit... never mind."

"Nah, say it. It's a bit what?"

"You know. It just... smells a bit *lived in,* in here. That's all."

"So, you tryna say I'm funky?"

"No, no. I'm not saying that. I'm just saying that your room has smelled better." She smiled.

"Girl, shut up!" I chuckled and playfully slapped her arm.

"I'm just keepin' it a buck with you, boo! That's all! Just light some candles in this bitch and spray a couple squirts of Febreze, and shit will be as good as new!"

"I appreciate that, and I also appreciate you being here. I know you didn't plan on staying out here this long."

"Yeah, I definitely didn't. But it's not like I was really out there doing anything life changing back at home. Besides, you need me. I can go back to substitute teaching anytime."

"Are you sure?" I asked.

"Yeah, I'm sure. You're my best friend, Raquel. I couldn't see myself being anywhere else right now but here with you."

I sighed and then looked at her. I figured since Law was gone, there was no need in me holding onto the real way we came across each other. It was time I started treating Camille like the best friend I knew she'd always been to me and told her the truth, the whole truth, and nothing but the truth, no matter how crazy it was going to sound.

"Camille... what would you say if I told you I hadn't been all the way honest with you?"

"About what?"

"About Law and I... and how we met."

"Why would you lie about something like that though?"

"I didn't lie. I—I just didn't tell you the whole truth."

"So, are you going to tell me now?" she asked.

"Yeah." I nodded. "I am."

"And you swear you're not going to leave anything out this time?"

"I swear."

"Pinky promise?" she asked, holding out her pinky finger.

"Promise pinkies." I nodded.

I wrapped my pinky finger around hers, and we both leaned in to kiss them.

"Okay, now spill it."

"So, you remember when I told you that there were things that you just wouldn't understand?"

"Yeah."

"And you remember how I told you that I met Law after he saved my life?"

"Yeah... so?"

"So, you remember the night that you, Shante, and I were all at the club? Well, after I left, I was headed back up to the room. I actually texted you guys when I got in the elevator and not in the room. I kicked off my shoes because my feet were killing me, and when I was on my way up to our floor, the elevator stopped, and there was a man lying there bleeding. It was... it was horrible. He was asking for my help and before I could say or do anything, I saw him get shot. I pulled out my phone, and instead of pressing the call button, I pressed the capture button and took a picture of the shit. The only thing I could do after that was run. I—I tried to call 911 when I got to the bottom floor, but as soon as I got outside, I was snatched up and thrown into the back of a car."

"Oh, my fuckin' God, Raquel! Are you serious? What the fuck? Was Law behind that shit? Did he kill that man?" she yelled.

"Please, Camille. Just let me finish."

"Hell no! No, Raquel! Fuck that! Are you telling me he was behind that shit? Just answer me that!"

"Just listen! Please!" I said, raising my voice.

"Fine," she said, throwing up her hands. "Go ahead."

"So, I was taken to this warehouse. I threw up. It was disgusting, but Law showed up. H—he took my phone, and..."

"Hold up. Didn't you call me that night to tell me that you were fine and that you weren't flying back with us because you met some nigga?"

"Yeah." I nodded.

"And you were with Law the entire time and not the nigga you met in the club?"

"Yes."

"Are you fucking kidding me, Raquel? Did this nigga hold you fuckin' hostage because of what you fuckin' saw him do?"

"Camille, you don't understand! He didn't do it!"

"So what if you think he didn't pull that trigger. He had something to do with it, right? Right!"

"Just let me fucking finish," I said sternly.

"I don't want to hear any more of this fucked up story, Raquel! Honestly! You painted this glorious picture of this man, had me in his house thinking that he really gave a fuck about you, when the whole time he was just keeping you around so that you wouldn't air his dirty fuckin' laundry to the fuckin' police! Are you kidding me, Raquel? I thought you were smarter than that! That nigga don't love you, Raquel!"

"Shut the fuck up, Camille! You don't know what you're talking about! You don't know him! You don't know shit!"

"I don't know that nigga. You're right about that, but I know niggas period, Raquel. All a nigga wants is a quick fuckin' come up. He saw you. He saw how beautiful you were and how vulnerable you were, and he took advantage of that shit, Raqi! He took advantage of you! He made you fall in love with him, but he didn't love you back! All this shit is fake! It's not real! It's a mothafuckin' façade or a mirage or whatever the fuck else, aight? Even though what you and Derrick had wasn't perfect, at least I can say the shit was real. You knew who that nigga was! He didn't trick you into shit! He didn't risk your fucking life! Shit! Now that I know all this shit, I'm glad he's dead!"

"Camille, just stop! Stop! Shut the fuck up and stop!" I yelled.

"No! I'm sorry, Raquel. I really am. I'm sorry that this happened to you, but I wouldn't be your real friend if I didn't tell you the cold, hard truth. Law isn't who you thought he was, and now that all this shit is over, you need to pack your shit and get on a plane with me as soon as possible and leave this whole nightmare of an experience behind, okay? No funeral, no last respects, nothin'. Let's pack our fucking bags and get the fuck out of Miami for good!"

I stood up and wiped my face. I could feel my blood boiling inside me. She had me ready to put my hands on her and kick her ass all the way out of Florida. A part of me thought that since she was my best friend, she would've understood, but I was wrong. I couldn't expect someone who hadn't been around from day one to understand or even appreciate what Law and I had. Yeah, the shit was crazy, but it was still love. It was our love. I loved him for who he was, and that was something Camille just couldn't see.

"Look, Camille, I didn't tell you any of this shit so that you could judge and point your mothafuckin' fingers, aight? Because I'm sure your hands aren't clean either. I loved Law more than I will ever love any other man that walks this mothafuckin' Earth. You hear me? I lost him! And I don't give a fuck if I knew him for thirty minutes, thirty days, or thirty fuckin' years, you will not disrespect him in my presence or in this house! Do you know what that man did for me? Huh? He saved me from getting raped by two fuckin' men in an alley! He protected me from damn near every fuckin' enemy of his that came my way since I've fuckin' been here! He put clothes on my back, bought me a car, and showed me what true love was. That man loved me, okay? He fuckin' loved me! Me!" I yelled, while drilling a hole in my chest with my index finger.

Before Camille could respond, there was a knock on the door then the doorknob turned. Law's mother was standing there. I didn't know how much she heard, but a part of me was grateful for her interruption.

"Raquel, do you have a minute?" she asked. "I'd like to speak with you... in private."

"I'll leave you two alone, and we can finish our talk later," Camille said as she looked at me and then back at Law's mother.

Instead of responding, I let out a loud huff of air, trying to calm myself down. My body was shaking, and I was trying not to throw Camille's ass over the balcony. Camille walked past Law's mother. Her eyes followed the back of Camille's head until the bedroom door closed, separating them. She walked over to me and took my shaking hands in hers.

"Come sit with me, Raquel."

I followed her back over to the couch to sit down and rested both our hands in her lap.

"How are you holding up?" she asked.

"I don't know. It's like I'm... I'm..."

"Numb?" she answered.

"Yeah, exactly. But that shit right there... I can't handle that type of disrespect right now," I said, shaking my head as my bare foot tapped the ground repeatedly.

"I didn't hear everything, but I heard some of your exchange, and I don't want to overstep, but I will say this. Only you and Law know what the two of you shared, and you two are the only ones that matter when it comes to your relationship at the end of the day. Everybody is not going to be happy for you all the time, not even your closest friends."

"Yeah, you're right." I nodded. "But enough about that. I just wanted to say that I'm sorry for not coming to check on you for these last few days. I've been so wrapped up in myself and what I've lost... I didn't stop to ask you how you're doing. I know this has to be ten times harder on you."

"It is very hard... excruciating. But I'm a firm believer that God has a plan. Besides, my mother told me that you'd never know what a broken heart felt like if you'd never loved."

I nodded and gave her a quick smile.

"Thank you. I'll try to remember that."

Law's mother leaned in to hug me as I fought the tears back. It seemed like every time I blinked, there was a fresh tear that formed.

"I just miss him so much." I sniffled.

"I understand, Raquel. I miss him, too. I've been in touch

with the funeral home we used to bury their brother and their father. Do you want to go with me to view the body before the service?"

"I don't think I can. I can't see him like that."

"I understand." She nodded. "I will take Blaze with me or go alone."

"I don't want you to go alone."

"No, no. It's okay. I've done this before. Unfortunately, too many times. You don't have to worry about a thing. I'll handle all his funeral arrangements. You just take all the time you need to get yourself together."

"Can I just request one thing?" I asked.

"What is it?"

"A closed casket. I'm not going to make it through the service if I see his face. I want to remember him smiling and just how he was before all this shit happened, not with a straight face and just lying there."

Law's mother stared at me for a few seconds and then nodded slowly.

"Okay."

"You know what? Give me twenty minutes. I want to go with you. I feel like I owe it to him, and I shouldn't be sitting here in the house, moping and feeling sorry for myself."

"Okay. I'll see you downstairs."

I threw on some clothes, pulled my hair into a messy, top knot bun, and then grabbed my purse. When his mother and I got to the funeral home, we sat down on the gold parlor couch by the front door and waited for the funeral director to greet us.

"Mrs. Calloway?" he asked.

We both turned around, and then I realized he was only talking to Law's mother. I scanned the man up and down. He looked to be in his late fifties or early sixties. His hair had started to gray, but I could tell that, when he was younger, he was probably good looking.

"Hi, Vincent."

"It's nice to see you again, but I just wish it was under different circumstances," he said as he held her hand in his.

"Yes, me too. My daughter-in-law and I wanted to come in today to talk about planning my son's funeral."

"Yes, of course. I've been expecting you." He nodded. "My sincerest condolences to you both."

"Thank you." I nodded.

"Yes, thank you," she added.

Law's mother and the funeral director got up to go to the back to view caskets, and I followed. The three of us discussed when and where we wanted Law's service to be, the type of casket he'd be buried in, closed or open viewing, and even if we were going to have a live singer or pre-recorded music. I had never thought of answering any of those questions before, especially not on the spot like that. I was happy Law's mother was there to help because I just felt useless sitting there. I was physically drained, and we'd only been there for thirty minutes. The only input I gave was to have a closed casket and to not bother with having a bunch of flowers. After that, I tuned them out. When Law's mother stood to shake the funeral director's hand, I stood as well.

"Are you ready to go?" she asked.

"I think I want to see him."

"Um, I don't think that's a good idea," she said.

"Yes. His body has not been prepared, and is not ready for viewing just yet," Vincent added.

"Okay. Well, can I just have a minute alone?" I asked.

"Of course. Please take all the time you need in the sanctuary. We'll be in the front if you need us," he said.

"Thank you." I nodded.

I walked into the dimly lit sanctuary and looked around. There were rows of white chairs all lined up facing the direction of where the casket would be placed. I sat in the middle row and leaned forward to bury my head against the chair in front of me. I held my stomach. I felt nauseous with regret that I hadn't told Law all the things I wanted to tell him before he died and all the things I should have told him, but I didn't. Maybe I was too scared, or maybe I was just trying to protect us both from the truth for as long as I could. I didn't know. My head lifted, and I let it fall backward toward the back of the chair as I looked up to the sky. I didn't want the tears to fall again, but they started before I got the chance to stop them. My chest hollowed as my tongue tried to find the words.

"Baby... it's uh... it's me. I uh... I don't even know what I'm doing. I don't even know if you're up in Heaven yet or what you're doing up there. Is the line long? I know how impatient you can be sometimes." I chuckled. "But I guess you know that since you've been gone, I haven't really been worth a damn to anybody. I just sit in the room and lay on your pillow and try to see you in my dreams whenever I do sleep. Truth is, I haven't really been doing too much of that either... but I guess you already know that, too. Damn, I feel like I'm talking in circles."

I closed my eyes and exhaled slowly as my lip quivered then started talking again.

"Why'd you have to leave me, baby? We were supposed to spend the rest of our lives together, and now, you're gone and it's just me. I don't think I can do this shit alone, baby. I swear, I don't. Living without you is harder than I ever imagined it would be. I didn't think I'd ever have to even deal with this shit until we were well into our seventies or eighties, you know? I need you back, and I need you back here now. Just please come back."

I sighed as I sniffled and wiped my eyes with the back of my hand. I tapped the back of the chair in front of me as I stood to my feet.

"I gotta go. Your mom is waiting on me. I just want to say that I love you, and I miss you, and I wish more than anything that you were still here with me."

I blew a kiss up to the sky and turned to walk out of the sanctuary.

* * *

Law

I stood in the backroom and listened to Raquel pour her heart out to me when she thought no one was listening but my ghost. It took everything in me not to come out and give her exactly what she wanted to put her worries aside, but I knew I had bigger plans for the both of us. I couldn't let my heart dictate every move I made. I stood in the back, shuffling my feet against the carpet until the funeral director came back to meet me.

"They're gone."

"Are you sure?"

"Yes."

"Did everything go well? Everything is all set up?"

"Yes. Your mother gave me the money, and I provided her with the death certificate and the fake autopsy report. Oh, and she wanted me to give you this," he said, handing me my phone.

"Thanks. So, when's my funeral scheduled for?"

"Two days from now." He sighed.

I could tell that he was uneasy about what we were trying to pull off, but I brushed it off and reached into my back pocket.

"Aight, bet. And as promised, here you go," I said, unraveling a wad of hundred dollar bills, handing him ten.

"Andreas... I mean, Law, are you sure you want to go through with this? I'm sure this isn't the only way."

"It's my way. Just know that I want this shit publicized in the newspaper like everyone else so niggas will know I'm dead. What-ever happens after that, just know I got you covered, Vincent."

He let out another loud sigh and nodded.

"Okay."

Vincent took the money while I slid the phone in my back pocket. I turned to leave out of the back to get in the car. All hell was about to break loose in two days.

* * *

Blaze

I hadn't been back to the house since Law died. I hadn't been checking in on anyone or answering anyone's calls besides my mother's and some of Heaven's from time to time. The only places I'd been were the penthouse in South Beach and the liquor store. It seemed like weed, pussy, and Hennessy were the only three things that took my mind off everything but only momentarily. I'd been oversaturating my body with so much liquor that I knew if my liver could talk it'd be like *"Nigga, what is you doin'?"*

When I finally pulled up to the house, I grabbed the half empty fifth of Hennessy from the passenger seat and got out of the car. As soon as I unlocked the front door, I looked around as I took a swig. Although I knew there were people there, it felt strange not having Law around anymore. The house looked exactly the same but felt empty as hell. As soon as my foot hit the bottom step, I looked up to see Raquel coming down them.

"Hey," she mumbled as she stopped midway.

"What's up?" I asked.

"Your mom and I planned the funeral today," she told me.

"Word. When is it?"

"It's in two days."

"Bet." I nodded as I took another sip.

"How... Um... How's Nevaeh?"

"She's cool. She was givin' me a lot of shit about everything at first, but she's good now."

"And the baby?"

"The baby is fine. I'ma try and go to her next doctor's appointment with her in a few weeks."

"That'll be nice." She paused.

"Yeah."

I took a second to look up at her, and I immediately wished I hadn't. Her face looked so whitewashed, and the heavy bags under her eyes told me that she'd been getting the same amount of sleep as me.

"Blaze, you know if you wanna talk, I'm here."

"I know." I nodded as I took another swig from the bottle.

When I pulled it from my lips, I realized I had about two swallows left before it was going to be empty, and I wasn't in the right state of mind to make it all the way back out to the liquor store to get a fresh bottle.

"Shit," I mumbled.

"There's a little more upstairs. I've been nursing a bottle for the past few days. Just drinking enough to put me to sleep, but that ain't really been helping much." She shrugged.

"Bring it here then."

Raquel nodded and turned to walk back up the stairs. I followed her and walked into my room. I stumbled over to my bed and fell across it. As soon as I closed my eyes, I could feel my body crashing down. The room started spinning as I held my chest. I could hear my liver yelling, *"Nigga, you done did it now!"*

"As much as you think you want this, I don't think you need any more right now," Raquel said from behind me.

"I'll be fine. I just drank a little... or a lot too much. I'll smoke a blunt, and it'll bring me right back around. It always does."

"Can I hit it with you?" she asked.

I slowly poked my head up from my comforter and looked back at her. I didn't know if she was serious or joking.

"Are you for real?"

"Yeah."

I sat up and pulled two blunts out of my pocket along with my lighter. I lit one and passed it to Raquel then lit the other one to smoke on my own. She put it up to her lips to take a puff at the same time as me. We both let the smoke fill our lungs and then blew it all out through our noses.

"You know... the first time I ever smoked weed was with your brother," she said.

"Oh, for real?"

"Yeah." She nodded. "He laughed at me because I couldn't stop coughing."

"That sounds like some shit he would do." I chuckled.

We passed the blunts back and forth between each other, just inhaling and trying to keep the vibe as chill as possible. I turned my attention to the view outside my window. Limbs of tree branches stretched across the window as a slight breeze shook them.

"I just can't believe it. I can't believe any of it," she said as she rubbed her puffy, red eyes.

I didn't know if it was because she was high or if she was about to cry. I was hoping it was because she was high. I wasn't emotionally or physically stable enough to deal with her tears.

"Me either," I mumbled. "Have you talked to my mom?"

"Yeah, earlier today. You haven't spoken to her?"

"Here and there, but not too much. I haven't talked to her

about how she's holding up or anything. I wanted to go down and check on her today, but I just gotta sleep some of this shit off first."

"I understand. She's coping I guess. I don't really know. It's a fucked up thing to say, but she's been through this before, so she's probably handling this better than the both of us."

"Hell yeah," I scoffed. "Too many fuckin' times."

I passed Raquel the small blunt. I could see her fingertips burning as she tried to hold onto it. It even burned her lips a bit when she tried to take a pull from it. She quickly pulled back and passed it to me.

"Here. I can't smoke this shit. It's too small."

"You ain't got no tweezers?" I asked.

"Tweezers? For what?"

"To hold the roach."

"Roach? Where?" she jumped.

I laughed and shook my head.

"That's what that's called right here in my hand. It's little and dark... like a..."

"Roach," she said, cutting me off. "Yeah, I got it now."

"You miss him?" I asked.

"Every day."

"Yeah, me too. I'm sorry about how all that shit went down though... at your wedding and shit."

"Yeah, it'll definitely go down as one of the days of my life I'll never forget, no matter how bad I want to. It's like a permanent fuckin' tattoo on my brain."

"Mmhm," I grumbled.

"Looks like all we've got now is each other."

"Looks that way," I agreed.

Raquel and I both sat on my bedroom floor in silence with our heads trapped inside the clouds. We were lost in the heat of it all, not knowing which way was up or what to say or do next. Nobody knew I blamed myself for Law's death. Nothing like that would've happened if I hadn't killed Damien. I could've prayed until I was blue in the face, but none of it was going to bring either one of my brothers back. No matter how much I scrubbed or how good I washed, Law's blood was on my hands for the rest of my life.

"Are you really okay, though?" she asked, pulling me out of my feelings.

I sighed and shook my head.

"Look, Raquel. I honestly don't know. Waking up every day and trying to face myself in the mirror is hard enough. I was the youngest out of the three of us, but even though I was the baby, I was the toughest, you know? I don't really know what to say to make you feel better because I don't know how to make myself feel better. I'm just doin' what I'm used to doing so I don't have to deal with none of this shit."

"It's okay. I don't know what to say half the time either. Today was the first day I've spoken since the church. I am sorry though. I don't know what it's like to lose a sibling, but if I've only loved Law for this short period of time, I can only imagine how you feel after knowing him your entire life."

"See? That's it right there. I don't want you to feel bad for me. I don't want your pity or kind words or condolences. Ain't none of that shit gon' bring him back. It's just time for me to stand on my own two feet, you know?"

"Yeah, I do. I'm sure he'd be proud to hear you say that."

"But look, Raquel. I know how much my brother meant to you, and I'm sorry I couldn't... that I couldn't save him."

"It's not your fault, Blaze," she said as she rested her hand on my shoulder.

"I don't really care what you say, Raquel. I mean, I know you tryna be nice and all that shit, but I ain't tryna hear nothin' you sayin' right now. I don't wanna talk about it anymore because I don't like feelin' weak. I don't even know why we started talking about this shit in the first place."

"Because it's the only thing on everybody's minds," she told me.

As true as her statement was, I didn't have time for that shit. The only thing on my mind was getting back at them niggas. Period.

"I'm not gon' be satisfied until those niggas are bleeding out and gasping for their last breath at my feet. And even then, that still might not be good enough," I mumbled.

Raquel sighed and nodded.

"I'm mad too. Believe me. A part of me wants to tell you to go find them and give me a gun so I can put a bullet in them too."

I looked at her from the corner of my eyes. Her eyes had gone from being red and swollen to foggy and dark like storm clouds.

"Wow."

"What?"

"I don't know. I guess I just never thought I'd hear you say that." I chuckled.

"Yeah, me either." She grinned.

"My brother really did have an effect on you."

"Yeah, he really did. More than anyone will ever know."

"Real talk, though. Can we just drop the shit where it is? I don't want shit to get too deep. We don't need to be buried in our feelings any more than we already are."

Raquel nodded.

"Fair enough."

"Rest assured, you ain't gotta worry about shit. Okay? I just want you to know that I'm gon' handle all of this. I'm gon' take care of this family, and I'm gon' make sure we come out on top."

"I believe you. Did I already ask you how Nevaeh was doing? I can't remember," she asked, shaking her head.

"Yeah, your high ass did. But, it's okay. She's okay. Still a little shaken up, but she's a big girl. She'll be fine."

"Things are really taking off between you two, huh?"

"Something like that. But we just doin' what we gotta do for the baby right now, you know?"

"I get it. So, uh… is it… awkward for you to have Camille still staying here with us?"

"Nah. I don't pay that shit no mind. I mean, I'm not tryna play your friend or anything, but it was what it was between us. Just a one-time thing, you know?"

"Yeah, I get it."

"Why? Did she say something?"

"Nope. No, she didn't."

"You sure?"

"Yeah, I'm sure. I was just asking for me. That's all."

"Oh, okay."

"Well, I'm gonna go lay down. This weed got me sleepy as hell."

"Maybe now you'll get a good night's sleep."

"Yeah, maybe so. Thanks for the talk," she said.

"No problem."

Raquel got up and closed my bedroom door behind her. I slowly got up and sat on the edge of my bed. The conversation between Raquel and I had sent a whirlwind of thoughts surging through my head. As much as I knew I should've stayed my ass right in the house, my heart and my pride wouldn't let me. Every moment I sat was another moment wasted on avenging Law's death. My mothafuckin' brother was dead, and I was going to make the streets cry blood. I stood to my feet and pulled my gun out from my nightstand drawer. I put it in my back pants pocket and walked into the bathroom. I splashed some cold water on my face and reached in the medicine cabinet to pop a Xan. I walked out of the bathroom to wash the pill down with a shot of Hennessey. As soon as I grabbed my keys, I was out the door. If niggas wanted me to be a menace, that's exactly what they were going to get.

* * *

Dallas

I stood in front of Darius's apartment door and knocked. It took a minute or two before I heard his footsteps marching toward the door. When he opened it, I looked him up and down. He was standing there in his boxers with no shirt on and his dreads thrown into a messy bun on top of his head.

"Nigga, what the fuck?" I asked.

"What's up? What you want?"

"Fuck you mean what do I want? You already know why the fuck I'm here, so stop playin'. We got business to discuss; real important shit."

"Aight, talk."

"Nigga, I'm not sayin' no more words to you until you go put on some fuckin' pants!"

"Nigga, this my house. I'll put on pants when I'm good and damn ready. Either you gon' talk now, or you gon' wait til' I go bust this nut right quick," he said unapologetically.

"You got a bitch in here right now?"

Darius stepped in closer to me as he nodded his head.

"You remember the school teacher bitch I told you about?" he mumbled.

"Yeah. What about her?"

"Just know a nigga about to add some new words to his vocabulary, aight? I'll be back. Make yourself at home and shit.

Oh, and you might wanna turn the TV up loud. These walls thin as shit, bruh."

Darius let out a loud laugh and turned to go back in his room. I rolled my eyes and plopped down on his sofa and turned on the TV. I made sure to follow his advice and turned the volume up to the max. I didn't want to hear my brother puttin' in work just like I didn't want to see him standing in front of me in his drawers.

I spent the next forty-five minutes flipping through channels until I'd finally settled on *White House Down*. Just as it started getting good, I caught a glimpse of the school teacher out of my peripheral.

"Hey." She waved at me as she threw her purse over her shoulder.

"What's up?"

I wasn't gon' front. She was a pretty brown thing with a nice body on her. Her titties sat up nice and perky in her white tank top, so I knew she didn't have a bra on. Her jeans looked painted on as she sashayed toward the door. I almost broke my neck turning to watch her walk away.

"I'm Dallas by the way."

"Hi, Dallas. I'm Olivia. It's nice to meet you."

"Nice to meet you, too. Maybe I'll see you around."

"Yeah, maybe you will," she said as she curved her juicy lips to smile at me.

Once the door closed behind her, Darius walked out.

"Is she gone?" he asked.

"Hell yeah she gone."

"Bruh, that bitch is crazy as fuck. Look at my arms and my fuckin' neck! She scratched me the fuck up! You would've thought I was back there fuckin' a tiger or some shit!"

"You ain't ready for a bitch like that if you can't handle a few scratches, nigga."

"Nah, fuck that. What she did was more than scratches."

"You should let me take her off your hands then," I suggested.

"She fine as shit, ain't she?"

"Hell yeah." I laughed. "Where you find her at?"

"Nigga, why you worried about her? You know if Shiya see you with another bitch, her ghetto ass gon' be the first one to swing on somebody. You know Shiya crazy as hell."

"Yeah, she was a crazy one," I said, rubbing my hand against the back of my neck.

"What you mean *was*? What, y'all beefin' again or somethin'? I swear y'all niggas fight like cats and dogs."

I blew hot air out of my nose and got up to walk over to the window in his dining room. The window was speckled with droplets of rain as it started to pour down outside. I knew it was time for me to come clean to him about what had really happened to Shiya.

"Look. There's somethin' I gotta holla at you about. It's about her..."

"What about her? You tell her we got her nigga yet?"

"Nah," I said, running my hands down my face.

"Why not, nigga? What? You scared of how she's going to react or somethin'?"

"I can't tell her because she's dead," I blurted out.

Darius's face went from cocoa brown to pure white. His mouth dropped open, and he put his hand over top of it to close it.

"What happened?"

"She came at me about gettin' at that nigga Law... just how she did with Wolfe. I wasn't really trying to make a big move like shootin' up the wedding and shit, but when I ran it by Pops, he was with the shit, so that's what we did. But before all that, she came at me like she ain't just wanna get back at Law for playin' her or whatever. She wanted to get back at his new bitch, too."

"Okay, and?"

"And so, I told her if we were gonna do it, we were gonna do it my way. If the road don't lead to money in my pocket at the end of the day, then I ain't tryna do it, you feel me? So I said let's get her, hold her ass for ransom, and dig in that nigga Law's pockets like how he tried to do us with that Alastair shit. She agreed, and we ended up catchin' her slippin' the night before her wedding at the grocery store. I grabbed her ass, threw her in the car, and we went down to the warehouse. All I wanted to do was hold her until I secured the bag, and then I ain't give a fuck about what happened to her after that.

I guess just seeing her made Shiya feel some type of way because she started going off track with everything I'd talked to her about. She really wanted to shoot the bitch. So, I start going along with the shit. I'm yellin' and tryna scare her to show Shiya that we ain't need to kill her. It was easy enough just to have her fear for her life instead of me actually puttin' a bullet in her. Well, Shiya wasn't fuckin' with that shit, nigga. She talkin' about some *'Dallas, give me the gun. I want to shoot this bitch myself.'* I'm like what the fuck? So then, the girl yells out that Law was Damien's half-brother."

"So that's how you found that shit out? From Law's girl? How the fuck did she know? Does that mean that nigga knew the whole time?"

"Nigga, I don't know. Just the words alone had my head so fucked up. I didn't know what to say. At first, I thought she was lying, but then she told me she had living proof."

"Who? The mom?"

"That's what I was thinkin'. Like, who the fuck else could it be? Then she confirmed that shit right then and there. She said Law, Wolfe, and Blaze, and fuckin' Damien were half-brothers, and Damien was the oldest!"

"What the fuck!" Darius said with his hands resting on top of his head.

"Exactly. So while I'm standing there trying to process this whole shit, Shiya reaches for my gun. I go to pull the gun away from her, and my shit went off."

"No."

"That shit eats me up inside every day, nigga. Every fuckin' day."

"Damn, nigga. Why didn't you tell me that shit when it first happened? You know I would've had your back. What did you do with her body?"

"I dumped that shit in the ocean."

"Hold up, nigga. You just went and dumped a whole body in the ocean by yourself?"

"Nah, I made Law's bitch help me. I knew she wouldn't go to the police if she was an accomplice. She'd be too scared to say shit to anybody. Plus, it wasn't like her and Shiya were best friends. Shiya hated that girl."

"Yeah. True."

"But that's not all. I forgot to tell you that her fuckin' ex-boyfriend or somebody showed up. He was at the grocery store and said he followed the car to the warehouse, so he helped with the body too."

"Then what'd you do with him? I know you just didn't let him walk away. Did you?"

"Nah. I shot that nigga in the back. I didn't kill him, though. I just had to make a point to her ass that if she snitched, she'd be the next one with a bullet in her."

"You ain't kill him? What if that nigga goes to the police?"

"He won't."

"How you know that?"

"He was just as scared as she was, if not more."

"And that's exactly why you should've killed him. Scared mothafuckas snitch!"

"I'ma tell you like I told her. If he ain't dead, I'll make him wish he was. He already knows what I'm capable of."

Darius sat on the couch and rested his head against the back.

"So, what the fuck happens now?"

"What do you mean?" I asked.

"I mean with everything. Are you gonna meet with the mom and get to the bottom of this shit with Damien to see if it's really true, or are you going to confront Pops about it, or what?"

"None of that shit is on my mind right now. We got other shit to discuss."

"About what? Law?"

"Yeah. His funeral is tomorrow, and Pops thinks tomorrow is going to be the time to run up on Blaze and take his ass out. Then we can wipe our hands with those niggas for good."

"Damn. First a wedding and now a funeral. Pops is getting ruthless in his old days."

"Hey. We do this shit, and we done. We gon' be back on top."

Darius nodded as he looked at me.

"So, what's the plan?"

"Aight, so here's what we're going to do..."

CHAPTER THREE

Raquel

It was the night before the funeral, and Blaze, his mother, Camille, and I were all sitting together in the living room. Blaze had a glass of liquor in his hand, while the rest of us sat around in silence, letting the noise from the television fill the room.

"Is anybody hungry?" Camille asked. "I was thinkin' we could get pizza or something so nobody has to cook."

"Nah. I'm straight. I got everything I need right here," Blaze said, pointing to his glass.

"We could do pizza. Is that fine with you?" I asked his mother.

"I haven't had pizza in years. But yeah, that's fine with me."

"Okay, cool. Any specific toppings?" Camille asked.

"Pepperoni," I told her.

"Okay, Raqi. I'm going to put the order in. You wanna ride with me to go pick it up?"

"Sure." I shrugged.

Camille and I hadn't really spoken since I told her everything about Law and me, so I knew that was why she wanted me to go with her to pick up the food. I damn sure wasn't in the mood to hear anything negative she had to say. And if she came at me sideways, I had no problem letting her ass have it again.

I tossed Camille my keys, and she got in the driver's seat and pressed the button to start the engine. As soon as she put the car in drive, she looked over at me.

"So, are we going to keep playing this game?"

"What game?" I asked.

"Don't play dumb, girl. You know exactly what I'm talkin' about."

"If you have somethin' you need to say, then say it, Camille. I already said everything I needed to say to you."

Camille sighed and nodded.

"You know what, Raqi? You a grown ass woman. You gon' feel how you wanna feel, and you gon' love who you wanna love, even if it's not the way I envisioned it for you. So, I'm woman enough to tell you that I'm sorry for how I reacted when you told me everything. You needed me to just listen and be your shoulder to lean on in that moment, and I overreacted. Law ain't never do nothin' to me personally. He let me come and stay in his home, so I could be with my best friend, and for that, I'm sorry for what I said about him. I shouldn't have disrespected him like that."

"Thank you, Camille. That really means a lot. I just want to be able to talk to you about anything without you judging and thinking you know the whole story, and you don't."

"I understand. But you gotta know that you're my best friend. I mean, put yourself in my shoes. If I was sitting there telling you all that about a man I met, you'd be lookin' at me like I had a second head growing out of my neck, and you know it."

I nodded.

"Yeah. You're probably right."

"Ain't no probably, bitch. I know I'm right."

"Whatever," I said, curling my lips to the side.

"So... we good?"

"Yeah. We good."

When Camille and I got back with the pizzas, we took them in the kitchen and put them on the counter. Camille grabbed a few slices and went upstairs, while I popped my head around the corner into the living room to let Blaze and his mother know that the food was ready. Blaze didn't move, but his mother stood up and followed me back into the kitchen.

"How many slices would you like?" I asked her as I reached into the cabinet to grab a plate.

"One slice is fine," she told me. "I don't want to overdo it with the medicine I'm taking. I don't know how good this pizza is going to agree with my stomach."

I put one slice of pizza on a plate for her and then fixed my own.

"I understand. How are you feeling today?"

"You know... you all ask me that a lot here... at least ten times a day. I'm just going to start giving you a thumbs up or down from now on, so you don't have to ask so much."

I blew air out of my nose as I smiled without laughing.

"Okay. So, are you having a thumbs up or thumbs down kind of day?"

She stuck out her thumb and turned it to the side then chuckled.

"Are you ready for tomorrow?" she asked me as she stood across from me.

"No. Not at all."

"The funeral is the hardest part believe it or not. After that, things get easier. You just have to take it day by day."

I nodded to her without responding. I'd buried the part of me that blamed her for all the drama because I'd been too focused on grieving over the loss of Law. As the days went on, it got harder for me to hide my true feelings toward her. I could feel it coursing through my veins and settling in the crevices of my bones to the point where I was about to explode. It was pissing me off how calm and relaxed she seemed through the whole ordeal. I guess I'd expected her to be falling apart at the seams like I was. Whatever it was, I wasn't feeling that shit.

"Is that what you do?" I snapped.

She looked up from her plate and gave me a surprised look. I knew she wasn't expecting the attitude in my voice.

"Yes. That's what I do. That's the only thing anyone can do, Raquel."

"And you can live with that?"

"What is this really about, Raquel?"

I sighed and chewed my bottom lip. I knew I was about to explode, and there was no stopping me. I stepped around the island that was separating us and made sure I spoke in a firm but low tone.

"You don't think you should've told them about your secret? About Damien? All of this could've been avoided. Maybe you would have three sons standing here today instead of having to bury another one tomorrow!"

My heart was pumping fast, and I didn't even have the desire to eat anymore. I was just so mad at her for all of her secrets and forcing me to keep them too.

"It doesn't matter now," she mumbled.

"Yeah. You're right. It doesn't because it's out," I blurted out.

"What do you mean it's *out*?"

"I mean, his sick ass ex and her boyfriend, who just so happened to be a fuckin' Price brother, tried to fuckin' kill me the night before my wedding! The only reason he didn't kill me is because I told him your secret!" I said through gritted teeth.

"You what?" she said as she drew back and slapped me across my face. "You don't know what you've done!"

"Yo, what's going on in here? What was that sound?" Blaze asked as I quickly turned my back to hold the side of my face.

"Do you want to tell him, or should I?" I asked.

I could see the panic in her eyes, but I didn't give a fuck. She should've never put her hands on me.

"Nothing is going on. Raquel and I were just having some girl talk. That's all," his mother told him.

"You sure?"

"Yeah. I'm sure. Isn't that right, Raquel?"

I cut my eyes at her and then quickly glanced at Blaze.

"Mmhm."

"Oh, aight. Don't mind me then," he said as he walked over to grab a slice of pizza and then left as quickly as he'd come.

"I'm sorry..." she whispered to me. "I shouldn't have done that."

She stepped closer to me and tried to touch my face, but I swatted her hands away.

"Don't you fuckin' touch me," I said, as tears stung my eyes.

I turned my body to fully look at her with disgust as I shook my head. I couldn't believe she'd put her hands on me. My own mother had never slapped me before, and I wasn't about to get slapped around by the woman who was supposed to have been my mother-in-law. To top it all off, she even had me lying about dumb shit to cover her ass. That's when I realized it wasn't her secrets that needed to be kept quiet. It was her lies.

"There's value in holding onto secrets, Raquel. Maybe you'll learn that one day."

"And maybe you'll learn that no matter how deep you try to bury the past or your secrets, that shit will always come out in the end," I said and stormed out of the kitchen.

* * *

The Next Day...

It was the day I never thought I'd see coming until Law and I were well into our seventies or eighties—his funeral. I found myself sitting at the kitchen island with a glass of Sprite fizzing in front of me, watching my salty tears drip into the glass one by one.

"C'mon, Raquel," Camille said as she popped her head into the kitchen. "The limo is outside to take us to the..."

"Don't say it. I know what today is."

"Okay." She nodded as she walked up and stood beside me.

I slowly stood to my feet and took my eyes down to the floor and looked at it as if it was falling out from underneath me. Camille grabbed my hand, and I followed her to the front door. I tightly clutched the door handle, not wanting to let go, not wanting to move, not wanting to face the events of the day that were ahead of me.

"Come on, Raqi. We're going to be late if we don't leave now."

"I don't care," I mumbled as I stared at the ground.

My eyes were swollen, and there were heavy, gray bags sitting underneath them. I hadn't gotten a good night's sleep in what seemed like an eternity. I hadn't had the desire or the energy to do my hair, wash my ass, or even brush my teeth, but Camille made sure I got it all done in time for the funeral. I was thankful she was still around. I didn't know how I would've made it through anything without her, especially since I wasn't speaking to Law's mother after the stunt she pulled. I was still livid to my core about that shit.

"I know you don't want to go. Nobody wants to go. What happened to Law... it was... well, it was tragic. I wouldn't wish that on my worst enemy."

I turned to face Camille with tears in my eyes.

"Oh, please don't cry, Raquel."

"I can't help it. It gets harder and harder to smile every day. I don't know what I'm doing. I'm just floating through life with no direction right now. Everything is cloudy like it's just all one big, bad dream that I can't wake up from, no matter how many times I pinch myself," I said as I wiped my face with the back of my hand.

I chewed my bottom lip to stop it from quivering. Tears started to flood the back of my eyes, causing pressure. I knew if I blinked once, they would fall right out. Camille squeezed my hand and tugged on my arm.

"You my best friend. You know that, right?" she asked.

"Yeah, girl. I know."

"You got this, okay? But if you don't want to go... Well, I understand that too, and I'll sit right here with you."

"No, I have to go. I wouldn't be able to live with myself if I didn't say my final goodbyes to him. I can't disrespect him and what we had like that by not showing up..." I paused. "You know... I remember the first day I saw him. Even though the entire situation of how we came together was crazy as hell, I knew I loved him. Now, I just feel like I'm just dying inside with every breath that I take. That shit isn't normal."

"Of course, it is, girl. You loved him and you're grieving. You have every right to feel what you're feeling right now. If you feel like you need to cry, then do it. If you feel like you want to scream, then do that too. I won't judge you. Scout's honor."

"Scout's honor? Camille, you were never a girl scout."

"So what? Shit sounds legit when you put that on the end of a sentence."

"Shut up!"

"I'm just saying... it does!" she joked.

"Whatever. Thanks for making me smile, girl."

"Always. You know I got your lil' light bright, almost white ass until the day I peace out of this bitch! But okay, let me draw the crazy back in for a second and be serious because this is some serious shit," she said as she exhaled and put both of her hands on my shoulders. "Look, Raquel. I know you're lost right now. I... I almost don't even have words for you. Just know that I'm here for you, okay? No matter what."

I smiled and nodded, and the two of us joined Blaze and his mother inside the limo to head to the funeral home. When we arrived, the first thing my eyes landed on were the bright red roses on top of his casket.

"I don't think I can do this," I whispered to no one in particular.

"Here. Take this," Blaze told me as he walked up beside me and handed me a small bottle of Hennessy.

I looked at the bottle, twisted the cap, and turned it up to my lips. Blaze and I went back and forth taking swigs to ease the pain. We took a drink for Law, for Wolfe, and because neither one of them should have been dead in the first place.

* * *

Blaze

I wiped the excess liquor from around my mouth and put the bottle away. I'd lost my father, Wolfe, Law, and I knew with my mother being sick, her last day probably wasn't far away either. My heart was more than broken over just the thought of it all. My heart didn't exist anymore. I lowkey felt like my eyes didn't get a chance to dry after losing Wolfe. Then to lose Law the way I did just hurt. It was like a bullet lodged in my chest that could never be removed. I never wanted to see my brother lying dead in a casket. I wished more than anything that I could've saved my brother, or even taken his place. The shit was fucking with me hard, but I knew I couldn't show any emotion.

All I wanted to do was go to the strip club and throw a few stacks at some big booty bitches or shoot up some shit, but I didn't do either. Instead, I sat in front of my brother's closed casket, praying my high would last through the rest of the service. Truth be told, I was paranoid as fuck, thinking about who was going to try my family next and why. I knew all the shit that I'd done would come back on me one day, but I just didn't know how. Because I had been so paranoid, I went out and copped two new guns. After that, I headed straight to the gun range to sharpen my aim. I was gonna make sure the bullets that I fired out of my guns were going to kill. I had three things in mind when I saw those Price niggas again. There would be no talking—only aim, shoot, and kill.

I stood up and rested my hand on my brother's gold casket and lowered my head.

"Why you have to leave me, bruh?" I whispered. "Shit ain't gon' be the same without you, but I promise you I'm gon' take care of everything. Rest in peace, my nigga. I love you."

I leaned down to kiss the top of the casket.

"Blaze," Camille said as she walked up beside me. "I know I haven't really spoken to you much, but I just wanted to say that I'm so sorry for your loss."

I glanced at her and then slowly shook my head at her like she'd just spoken a foreign language to me.

"My loss? You wouldn't know the half."

I brushed past her and went to sit beside my mother. I threw my arm around her as she sat quietly, staring at the casket.

"How are you holding up, Ma?" I asked as I kissed her cheek.

"I'm making it."

"How are you feeling, though? In any pain?"

"No more than usual."

I noticed she was keeping her answers short, and I figured it was because of the stresses of the day, so I let it go.

"Shit fucked me up... losing him like that," I said to her.

"Yeah. I know. But you'll be fine, baby," she said, patting my hand. "Everything will be fine."

"I hope so, but I don't know. It still feels like a bad dream sometimes."

"Listen to me, Blaze. Everything is going to be fine. These things... they have a way of working themselves out in the end."

I found myself looking around the small funeral home every few minutes, watching for anything that seemed off. I knew the Price brothers thought they had one up on me now that Law was gone. I also knew that I was the final target on their to-do list, and they weren't going to catch me slipping. If they could shoot up a wedding, they damn sure wouldn't have a problem shooting up a funeral. I'd had a fluttering feeling in the pit of my stomach for days like some shit was going to go down. And if it did, me and the pistol concealed on my side were going to be ready.

When the funeral started, the choir sang "Going Up Yonder," which was the same song they sang at both my father and Wolfe's funerals. I glanced over at Raquel, who was leaning on Camille's shoulder with a tissue glued to her trembling hand. Her nose was red and so were her eyes. I shook my head. Just before the pastor started the eulogy, I heard the doors open. I quickly turned around with my hand glued to my side, ready to bust slugs.

Lo and behold, Darius and Dallas Price were standing there. I pulled my gun out of the holster, took the safety off, and started firing in their direction with no questions asked. I fired three bullets and saw two fly past me from behind me. In the midst of the service, the tears, and the songs, stood my brother—alive and busting his gun right beside me.

It wasn't a secret that niggas wanted me dead. As far as they knew, they'd gotten what they'd come for. I was no longer a threat to them. Since I was out of the picture, I knew it would only be a matter of time before they came for Blaze, and I knew they would do it when they thought he'd be most vulnerable—my funeral. I needed my brother to be ready, and with a so-called baby on the way, I honestly didn't know if he would be. I was relieved to see I was wrong. He was shooting bullets through the air right along with me.

My pops always said that niggas only cared about you when you were six feet under. Those niggas had left me for dead and were ready to dance on my grave if they were ever given the chance. Because I knew they were praying on my downfall, I would never sleep on them how they slept on me. Sleeping on your enemies is what gets you put six feet under, and I wanted to be on top of everything, especially the ground.

Once they saw me standing there, their eyes glazed over as if they'd seen a mothafuckin' ghost. My bullet pierced Darius, and he fell back while Dallas turned to run for cover. When the gunfire stopped, I stood tall and looked Raquel in the eyes.

"L—Law?" she mumbled with her eyes wide as saucers.

"It's me, baby. I'm back."

Instead of responding, I watched her eyes cross as she collapsed to the ground.

CHAPTER FOUR

Raquel

His words hit me like a bus. They were like the sound of a smoke alarm during a fire. I felt like it was all one big hallucination until I woke up on the ground with Camille hovering over me, fanning a program in my face.

"Oh my God, Raquel. Are you okay?" she asked.

"I—I'm okay," I whispered as I looked around for Law to see if I had just made the last ten minutes up in my head. My skin was hot, and I felt pain in my cheeks.

As soon as my eyes landed on his, my heart skipped a beat. I felt like I was falling off a cliff, trying my best to claw and hold on.

"Law? How the fuck?" I mumbled.

"It's me," he said as he grabbed my hands and pulled me off the ground and into his arms.

I couldn't believe Law was alive and holding me. My body shook with chills at the simple touch of his fingertips. I didn't want to get too excited because there was a part of me that still didn't believe it was real.

"Pinch me," I whispered into his chest.

"What?" he chuckled.

"I won't believe any of this shit until you pinch me."

"How about I kiss you instead?" he asked as he put both of his hands on the side of my face and pulled my lips onto his.

I could feel my knees buckling underneath me. I was truly

living the fairytale love story I always wanted. It was just the hood version.

"It's really you," I said as tears streamed out of my eyes.

For the first time since my wedding, I could say that I was actually crying tears of joy. I held the sides of his face and then wrapped my arms around his neck. I made a promise to myself that I was never letting go of Andreas Calloway ever again.

"How? How did you do any of this?" I asked unable to wrap my head around it all.

Law stepped back and glanced over at his mother.

"Hold up. You knew the entire time?" I asked her.

"My son asked for my help, and that's what I gave him," she told me.

Law looked back at me and flashed me an apologetic smile. I sighed. A part of me felt bad for coming at her the way I did, but in my defense, I didn't know the little secret she had with him, and it still didn't give her the right to put her hands on me. I had so many questions running through my head at the time. So much of me was just happy that I'd gotten another chance at my happily ever after with him, but I'd be lying if I said that a part of me didn't feel betrayed. There were too many secrets standing in between our happiness on his part and mine.

Law looked back at me and flashed me an apologetic smile. I

* * *

It felt good to hold Raquel in my arms again, but I couldn't live in that moment with her for too long. I still had business to handle. I'd turned the tables and was back in the position to make moves. It was time to let everybody know, starting with Darius. Blaze and I walked over to Darius, who was laying on his back, clenching his stomach.

"He ain't dead. You want me to finish him off?" Blaze asked as he aimed his gun at him.

"Nah. Stand his bitch ass up. Call the crew and take him to the warehouse. I got somethin' in mind for his ass."

"Man, fuck you, nigga!" Darius yelled out as blood spewed from inside his mouth. "I ain't throwing no flags, nigga. I don't give a fuck what you do to me. You want me? You gon' have to take me alive!"

"Fuck me, huh?" I asked as I drew back and landed a punch straight into his ribs.

I could hear his bones rattle loose inside him. Darius screamed out in pain and doubled over. I watched blood drip out of his mouth onto the carpet as he howled.

"Meet me there in twenty," I told Blaze.

Blaze put his gun back on his holster and pulled Darius off the ground by his dreads. His screams pierced my ears again as he dragged him out of the funeral home. I turned back to look at Raquel.

"I'll see you at the house later."

When we got to the warehouse, a few of my goons helped Blaze tie Darius up. His breathing was sketchy, but he was still conscious. I stared at him and shook my head.

"Fuck you lookin' at, nigga?" he managed to get out.

I could tell he'd already lost a good amount of blood, but I didn't give a fuck. I wanted his ass to suffer. Most importantly, I wanted to send a message to Dallas that his days were numbered. I stood over Darius and shook my head.

"You about to get killed all while trying to kill me, nigga. Now if that ain't karma, I don't know what is." I smirked as I pulled a blade out of my pocket.

"If you gon' kill me, then kill me, nigga. I ain't afraid to die! I ain't scared of a mothafuckin' thing!" he yelled and then spat his blood onto my shoes.

I looked down at my shoes and then back up at Darius.

"What finger did you use to pull the trigger?" I asked.

"What the fuck are you talkin' about nigga?"

"When you put that bullet in me. What finger did you use?"

"Man, nigga, fuck you!"

"Fair enough." I nodded. "Blaze, hold out this nigga's hands."

Blaze walked over and grabbed Darius's right wrist.

"Don't ball up your fist now, pussy ass nigga," he told him.

When Darius didn't loosen his fingers, I shook my head and drove my blade down into his hand and pulled it right back out.

"Ahhh," he yelled out in pain, and then all five of his fingers stuck straight out.

"Next time, listen to what the fuck niggas tell you to do," I said and sliced off his right pointer finger.

"Man, fuck!" Darius yelled with tears rolling down his face.

"Hold out is other hand, Blaze," I told him.

Blaze walked over and held out Darius's left wrist and instead of balling up his fist, he let his fingers hang limp as I sliced off his left pointer finger. The sounds of Darius' screams were like music to my ears. I could've listened to him suffer all night, but I knew I had other shit to do. I stepped back and took my gun out from behind my back. Blaze stepped out of the way as I aimed my gun at his forehead.

"Tell your brother we said hello," I told him and sent a bullet straight through his skull.

"Fuck!" Blaze groaned.

"What?"

"I moved all the way out of the way, and I still got this nigga brain pieces on my shit," he said, looking down at his pants and shoes.

I chuckled. It felt so fucking good to be back in the position of power. From that moment on, Dallas and I had a score to settle with one another. We were both one for one. He'd killed Wolfe, so Blaze killed Damien. Now that Darius was dead, there was only one left. I was ready to go to war with that nigga and let my soul bleed.

* * *

Blaze

I stared at Darius's blood on the ground and smiled.

"One down; one to go."

"Hell yeah," Law said as he dapped me up.

Law and I looked at each other at the same time, and I shook my head. A nigga was fucked up on the inside just looking at him standing and breathing, when an hour ago, I was kissing the top of his casket. When I found out my mother was in on the shit, I didn't know how to feel. It was clear our family was full of secrets, and my mother was the vault that held them all in.

"Blaze, look..." he started.

"Nah, stop the conversation right there, nigga. You ain't gotta explain shit. Whatever happened, never fuckin' happened, aight? I'm just glad to have you back."

Law pulled me into him and kissed my forehead.

"Just know I got a plan, and I'm gon' make sure we come out on top, aight?"

"I trust you, my nigga, more than I trust anybody in this world."

"I am my brother's keeper."

"Always." I nodded.

* * *

Raquel

The choice between being a good girl and a smart one shouldn't have been a question, but it was. It seemed like the moment Law whisked himself back into my life, he was gone again. I was left with my mouth and my heart sitting wide open. When I returned to the house, I took a shower then sat in my towel and waited for him to come home. No matter how much I wanted to hide it, the more time I spent waiting on him, the more resentment built up in my veins because he didn't let me in on his plan. Law had ruined my fairytale wedding for his own selfish desires. Everything I'd ever known about being a good girl had flown out the window the moment I met Law, so the only choice I had left was to be smart. He needed to know how I felt and that I wasn't going to be run over and pushed to the side anymore because he thought I couldn't handle things. I'd been through more than he even knew.

When the doorknob turned, I snapped out of my thoughts and looked him up and down.

"Hey," he said.

"You have blood on your shoes," I told him.

Law looked down at his shoes then took them off and walked toward the bathroom. Before I got another word out, I heard the shower turn on. I got up to walk inside the bathroom. His clothes were laying in a pile on the floor, hiding his blood-stained shoes.

"Where have you been?" I asked.

"You know where I've been, Raquel."

"Is he dead?"

Law pulled back the shower door and looked at me. He didn't bother to open his mouth. He didn't need to. I already knew the answer.

"Did you kill him?" I asked.

I stood there watching him uncomfortably as he surveyed my face. I pulled my towel closer to my body and shifted my weight from one foot to the other.

"Well, did you?"

"Yes," he said without emotion.

My lungs filled with air as I slowly inhaled. I didn't know whether to be happy he'd gotten his so-called revenge or to be upset that not even after the shit show of a funeral he had, he was already taking lives.

"You wanna join me?" he asked.

"No. I wanna talk."

"Talk to me about what?" he asked as soap ran down his body.

"You... me... all this shit," I said, raising my hands in the air and making circles with them.

"Come in here and talk to me then."

"Nah. I'll uh... I'll just wait until you get out."

"You sure about that?" he asked, stroking his dick as he eyed me.

I watched the soap rush down his dick as droplets of water

nosedived off the tip. I could feel my mouth salivating as I licked my lips. Against my better judgment, I dropped my towel and stepped inside the shower with him. Law turned to face me and pressed his lips and his dick against me.

"Law, stop. Seriously, I want to talk to you."

"I missed you, Raquel." He smiled.

His smile was perfect. Just seeing it used to make me smile, but I was trying so hard to be mad at him. Standing my ground became harder to do by the second. I just couldn't deny him.

"Yeah, I missed you as well... probably more than you'll ever fuckin' know."

Before I got a chance to say anything else, Law pulled me in front of him and lathered the front of my body with soap as he massaged my breasts. My nipples were getting harder by the second. My spine shivered as his wet hands started to glide down my thighs. He gave them a tight squeeze and then brushed his fingertips across my pussy.

"Mmm."

Law reached up to pull the shower head down and held it against my pussy. The warm water against my soft skin made my body tingle all over. He kissed the back of my neck then walked around me to bend down and suck on my left nipple as the water vibrated against my clit. I sucked in air through my teeth and slowly let my head fall back.

"Does that shit feel good?" he asked.

"Mmhm."

"Tell me how good it feels."

"It feels really good, baby."

Law put the shower head back on the hook and pulled me into his arms. He slid his tongue inside my mouth and then spun me around. He pressed my breasts against the glass as he reached around and rubbed my throbbing clit.

"Mmm... Law."

"Turn around and sit on the bench," he whispered in my ear.

I quickly appeased him and took a seat on the wet bench at

the back of the shower. Law dropped to his knees, pushed my legs up toward my head, and stuck his tongue inside my pussy. I locked my arms underneath my knees as I watched him suck and lick my sweet spot. Beads of water were jumping off the top of his head and dripping down his body.

"Oooh, fuck!" I squealed, expanding my lungs.

I reached down and palmed the back of his head as his lips explored my body. I could feel myself about to cream all over his soft, wet lips.

"Mmm... Don't stop, baby. Right there! I'm about to cum!"

"Cum on daddy's tongue, Raquel."

"Ooooh! Shittttt!"

Law stood to his feet, picked me up, and pressed me against the cold shower door. He slid his tongue inside my mouth as his fingertips traveled across my body like a road map.

"Mmm. You want this dick, Raquel?" he asked as he rubbed his hard, wet dick against my pussy.

I took his dick in my hand and stroked it as I looked in his eyes.

"I want you to beat this pussy up like it owe you money."

Law spun me around and pushed his hard dick in between my thighs to enter my pussy from the back.

"Mmm. Shit," I moaned as he instantly filled me up.

He picked me up and started fucking me standing up. My pussy glided up and down his rod as he had me suspended in the air.

"Goddamn, you creamin' on daddy dick already."

He put me back down on the floor and lifted my leg up to dig deeper into my tight pussy. I put both hands against the steamy glass as he continued to fuck me. I looked back at him and rested one hand on his shoulder. Law's hand glided up and down my stomach as he held me tighter.

"Shit! I wanna taste your sweet ass pussy again," he said in my ear as he kissed it.

Law pressed my back against the shower door, kissed down

my stomach, and lifted my right leg over his shoulder. I massaged his shoulder as he lightly flicked my clit with his tongue.

"Mmm. Just like that," I said, licking my lips.

I thrusted my hips forward to bump my clit against his tongue. Law reached up and grabbed my nipple as soap bubbles slid down my stomach.

"Oooh. Shit," I said as I grabbed the back of his head and glided my pussy up and down his face.

I reached out and rested my hand against the shower wall closest to me and let my other hand glide down his arm as he rubbed my breasts. I was determined to ride his face until I came again.

"Yes! Right there, baby! Lick my pussy just like that!" I squirmed.

Two tongue flicks later, Law had my eyes rolling in the back of my head as my body quivered from the crazy ass orgasm. Law turned me around so that my body was facing the back of the shower so he could bend me over better. He rubbed my ass, smacked it, and spread my ass cheeks apart to slide his finger into my asshole while his dick fucked my pussy.

"Oh shit, baby. Hold up!" I squealed.

"Take it, or I'm gon' put my dick in there, Raquel. You gon' take it? Huh? You gon' let daddy keep his finger in your ass?"

"Mmhm. Yes," I whimpered.

"That's my girl," he said as he continued to stroke me.

After a few more strokes, he pulled his dick out of my pussy and sat down on the bench. Law pulled me backward onto him so that I could ride his dick reverse cowgirl. I looked back and pulled his lips onto mine as I eased back onto his dick.

"Mmm. Shit, Raquel," he groaned.

He squeezed my nipples and smacked my breasts as I clamped my pussy around his dick. I put my finger in my mouth and sucked on it then dropped it down between my legs and rubbed my pussy.

"Yeah, that's it. Let daddy see you rub that juicy ass clit," he said as I bounced up and down on his dick.

Law ran his hand up my neck and gently grabbed my throat, slamming me down against him. I was screaming so loud he moved his hand from my throat to cover my mouth. His dick felt so good to me that I bit him.

"Ow, Raquel. What the fuck?" he said, snatching his hand away.

"I'm sorry, baby. Just don't stop!" I moaned.

He pulled both of my arms behind my back as he leaned my body forward to beat my pussy up. I could feel what seemed like my hundredth orgasm surfacing.

"Ahhh! Shit, baby, yesss!"

After I came, I turned to face him and sat back on his dick. He wrapped his hands around my small waist as I vigorously bounced up and down. I grinded on his dick so hard that my wet breasts were smacking against each other. My hair was soaking wet, dripping down my back, as he reached back to pull it.

"Mmm. Shit!"

"You like when daddy pull your hair, baby?"

"Yes, baby. I love it!"

I rubbed my hands all over his slippery chest as he sucked on my nipples. Law put both hands underneath my ass and pulled my pussy down deeper onto his dick so I could feel every inch of him pushing into my intestines.

"Oooh! Fuck!" I said, digging my nails into his shoulders.

Law rose to his feet with his dick still inside me. He pushed my back against the shower glass and stroked my pussy until it was sore. Law came inside me twice, and we continued to fuck until the water got ice cold. He handed me my towel from the floor and then wrapped one around his waist.

"Yo."

"What?" I asked, reaching for another towel to dry my hair with.

"I can't believe you bit me." He chuckled.

"My bad." I laughed. "I got caught up in the moment."

When I opened the bathroom door, I shivered. Law scooped me into his arms, carried me to the bed, and laid beside me.

"So, what did you want to talk about?" he asked.

"You think you slick and you not. A lil' dick down was not gon' make me forget everything that's on my mind."

"My dick is far from little, baby. But you already know that." He smirked.

I sighed and rolled over on my right side to look at him.

"I'm serious though, Law. I'm happy that you're back, and that was one hell of a welcome home reunion we just had. But still, is this how it's going to be when we're married? Huh? You makin' moves without me? Making decisions without me? We're supposed to be a team, Law. You and me! It's not about just you anymore, baby. It's about us."

"I know that, and I knew this shit was coming, but the only thing I can do now is apologize to you."

"I get that, but I just don't think that's good enough." I shrugged.

Law sat up and rolled off the bed to start putting on a fresh pair of clothes. He walked into the closet and then popped his head back out.

"Why the fuck can't you see everything I did, I did it for us, Raquel? Huh?"

"For us? How?" I asked as I slid on my bra and a pair of panties.

"Look at me, Raquel. You see me standing here. You see the life in my eyes and the blood running through my veins. It's me. I did this shit so that you and I could be together. I got one down and one more to go and then Shiya, and it's all over, okay? I'll be right back on top."

"There it is right there. You just said it!" I said, pointing in his direction.

"Said what?"

"This shit is still all about you, Law! There ain't no space for me in this big ass picture you've got painted in your head!"

"You don't see how hard I'm fightin' for this shit, for everything to be right so a nigga can fuckin' breathe easy again without a mothafucka tryna tear me down all the time!"

"Well, heavy is the head that wears the fuckin' crown," I told him.

"What the fuck is that supposed to mean?"

"It means that you need to see this shit from my eyes. Take a minute and stand in my fuckin' shoes, Law. I got fuckin' Camille breathing down my neck, asking me what was up and to tell her what was going on, and I couldn't say anything. I couldn't say shit!"

"I know your friend hates to see you crying because of me. I hate that shit, too, Raquel. Believe it or not, I do."

"I just don't understand why you felt the need to leave me out in the cold and treat me the way you did. Like I can't handle a fuckin' secret. That's all I been doing since I fuckin' got here, holding in everybody's fuckin' secrets! I just wanna know where shit went wrong. Like, what happened that you felt like you couldn't trust me? Tell me that! I deserve that!"

"You're absolutely right, and I know you do. I just... I just thought that this was the best way for me to handle the situation."

"And that's just not good enough for me, Law. I'm sorry, but it's not. I love you. I love the shit out of you, but I lost all my respect for you over this shit! It's all gone."

"Raquel..."

"No! You listen to me! You fake your death and you come back from the fuckin' grave, playing everything off all nonchalantly like that's just some shit niggas do every day, and it's not! No! Fuck that! I don't deserve that, and you know it!" I said as I pursed my lips together to stop the tears from falling out of my eyes.

"So, no matter what I say to you, I'm wrong?"

"Hell yeah! You were fuckin' wrong!" I yelled as I pulled a shirt over my head and buttoned my jeans.

"So, I'm wrong for wanting to be with you? For wanting us to make it? This is the only fuckin' way I knew how to do this shit, Raquel! Aight? That's what the fuck I'm tellin' you right now!"

We both huffed and stared at each other, chewed our bottom lips, and stared. The unspoken weight of words laid heavy on both of our tongues, but neither of us said anything. A part of me looked at Law like he was the hardest lesson I'd ever have to learn, but on the other hand, he was also the love of my life. Our love was a curse—a beautiful curse.

"You ain't nothin' but a fuckin' liar! That's just the type of nigga you are, huh? If you really want me like you say you do, then you wouldn't leave me in the dark like that!"

My emotions were pure and raw like freshly burned skin as I started running around the room, throwing clothes into an overnight bag. Law just stood to the side and watched me. I walked over to the nightstand and pulled my phone off the charger and threw it in my purse then I looked up at him.

"You wanna hear me say it? Huh? Law? Do you? I wasn't built for this type of shit, okay? There! I said it!"

"You think I don't know that shit, Raquel? I know!" he yelled and then paused.

"Look, I'm not trying to do this back and forth shit with you anymore, aight? I'm not with the tit for tat bullshit. I see through all that shit you pumpin' my way right now. You said it yourself; a nigga got your heart, Raquel. Ain't no need to front. I told you I'm sorry, and I'll keep tellin' you that for as long as it takes. All I want to know is do you forgive me?" he asked in a calmer tone.

"I don't think I can forgive you, Law... at least not right now."

I never thought in a million years that I would say those words and mean them, but his world was just too much for me. I couldn't take all the secrets and the lies. It was taking a toll on me mentally and physically. Being Law's queen came with a heavy crown for me to wear, a crown that was heavier than I'd ever imagined. His world was swallowing me whole.

* * *

Law

The look in Raquel's eyes was sincere, and for the first time, it made me nervous that my actions had pushed her to the edge. The very thing I had been trying to save seemed to be slipping away right in front of me.

"You don't mean that."

"I do. I'm done with all of this shit, Law. I'm done with the secrets, the lies, all of it. You can have this shit! What did I tell you, huh? I told you from the beginning that all I wanted was a watered-down version of you! That's it! Not all this other bullshit! You just don't understand how fucked up I was over this shit. I planned a funeral for you! I thought you died on our fucking wedding day, Law! How could you put me through this shit and just think an '*I'm sorry*' is good enough? It's not."

"So, you really done? Just like that? I thought you were loyal," I said, shaking my head.

"And I thought you loved me more than all of this status and power shit, but I was wrong. I was dead fucking wrong."

"Look, Raquel. I'll never tell you or anybody else what I'm thinking. That's when shit gets messy, aight? I'm sorry, but I handle my business how I handle *my* business. I knew how I wanted shit to go down, and I couldn't let you know shit. I didn't even let my brother know shit! It wouldn't have worked if you did. But look, if you really out, then the next time you tell a nigga you loyal, make sure your actions show that shit because words don't mean a mothafuckin' thing."

"How about before you tell a bitch you love her, you make sure you know what the fuck that word really means," she said as she threw her engagement ring at me and walked toward the door with a bag in hand.

"Raquel, put that shit down and come back over here. You goin' through all this shit and packing a bag for what? Just stop and calm down."

"No, Law. Let me go. I just need to be alone."

"Be alone?"

"Yeah, nigga. I need space away from you and time to think."

"Time to think about what?"

"About *my* next move," she said as the door slammed behind her.

I stood there with my mouth hanging wide open. Through the entire argument, I thought she was bluffing, but when that door slammed, reality hit me like a ton of bricks. I didn't see how we could go from me dicking her down to her packing a bag and getting ghost on a nigga. I wanted to tell her to stop, to stay, not to leave me. All those words were on the tip of my tongue, but my pride held onto them and nothing came out. My feet felt like they'd turned to stone, and I couldn't move. All I could do was replay the argument in my head over and over again. Emotionally, I kept everything I was feeling under wraps. That was the difference between Raquel and me. She wore her shit on her sleeve, and I hid mine inside the darkest parts of myself.

Deep down, I knew that Raquel was probably ten times better off without me. She deserved a nigga with a regular nine to five and a retirement plan, not a killer, not a savage, not somebody who had to worry every single day if each breath they took would be their last. I never wanted to get her that deeply involved in my world. That was something that knocked on my conscious daily. I felt bad for tainting her the way I did, but as bad as I felt, I couldn't picture myself without her.

Raquel had never lied or tried to run game on me. I respected her for that. After all, that's what made a nigga fall in love with her from the very beginning. Anything I'd lost in the past, I could get it back, except her. Raquel was really gone, and it didn't look like she had any intentions on coming back. I knew I was going to have to do some shit that I'd never done before to make her see that I loved her, and I was sorry. I just didn't know what. The only thing I could do was go to her with the hole in my heart and see if she would patch me up. I didn't care what I had to do. I had to get my girl back.

CHAPTER FIVE
Dallas

I was laid up in my bed with Olivia, the smart bitch my brother was fucking, smoking an L. I was staring at her ass sticking out of my silk bedsheets as she slept. I even thought about going for another round before the sun came up until my phone vibrated on the nightstand. I put the blunt in the ashtray, and I rolled over to grab my phone. It was a text message from a number I didn't recognize.

> 305-799-9999: Open up

I screwed up my face as I read the message over and over. Just when I was about to put the phone down and roll over, the front door to my apartment was kicked in.

"Oh my God! What the fuck was that?" she screamed.

"Shut the fuck up and stay here," I told her as I grabbed my gun out of the nightstand and ran toward the front door.

I stopped dead in my tracks when I saw my door hanging halfway off the hinges, and my brother's dead body lying in the opening.

"No... no... No! No! No!" I yelled as I fell to my knees in front of him.

"Dallas, what—" she said as she came around the corner.

She finished the rest of her sentence with a scream. I looked back at her. She was standing there, naked, and trembling with her hand over her mouth.

"What... what... is that? Da... Darius?"

I wiped the tears that were stinging my eyes and shook my head as I dropped my gun beside me and held my brother in my arms.

"Dallas! Talk to me! What the fuck is going on! I'm going to call 911!"

"No!" I yelled.

"Dallas, you've got to tell me something! I think I'm going to be sick!"

"Bitch, put your clothes on and get the fuck out!" I yelled.

Without saying another word, she ran back into my bedroom. A few minutes later, she ran out with her shirt hanging open and her jeans and heels on.

"I don't know what type of fucked up shit this is, but you need to call the fucking police, Dallas!"

I raised my gun and looked at her with a sinister look in my eyes. I quietly aimed my gun at her and cocked it.

"Get the fuck out. Now."

She stepped over Darius's body and ran out of my apartment. I pulled his body all the way into my apartment and slammed the door behind her. It didn't even close all the way, but anything was better than nothing. I didn't need mothafuckas I didn't know all in my business. I sluggishly walked back into my room and picked up my phone to call the number that texted me. The phone rang three times before someone picked up.

"How does it feel?" they asked.

"You think this shit is a joke, mothafucka?"

"The Calloways send their condolences," they said and hung up.

"Ahhhhhhhh!" I yelled out as I threw the phone against the wall.

I watched it fall to the floor. I couldn't believe my brother was gone. I felt like a coward for running out on him the way that I did, and I was forced to live with my decision. There was no turning back. I crawled over to the wall and wiped my wet eyes against my arm. I knew it was time to call my father and tell him what I'd been avoiding. I put the phone on speaker as I rested my head against the wall.

"Hello?" he answered.

"He ain't dead."

"Who?"

"That nigga, Law. He ain't dead, Pop."

"Where's your brother?"

I gritted my teeth against my bottom lip and let the silence answer for me as more tears escaped from the corners of my eyes.

"Dallas?"

"They got him, Pop. They busted in here and dropped his body on my fuckin' floor."

My voice broke like glass against a wooden floor when I said those words.

"What the fuck! How in the fuck could you let this shit happen?"

"I know, man. I know. I know I fucked up, aight? I know! You don't have to tell me what I did wrong, Pop! I feel it! I feel all of this shit right now!" I yelled into the phone.

"Your brother's blood is on your hands for this shit, Dallas! Yours!" he yelled.

"It's your fault all our blood is being spilled anyway!" I yelled back.

"What the fuck are you talking about?"

"You know exactly what the fuck I'm talkin' about! This whole time! Our whole lives ain't been shit but a fuckin' lie, and it's because of you! Damien's blood and Darius's blood is on your hands, and if they kill me, mine will be too!"

"Dallas, I may be old, but I'm not above whoopin' your black ass! Show some respect! I'm still your mothafuckin' father!"

"And what the fuck am I to you, huh? Huh? A fuckin' pawn

just like your other two sons? Fuckin' face it, nigga. I'm all you got left, and you need to start givin' me some answers!"

"Answers about what?"

"Answers about who Damien's real fuckin' mother is, and why the fuck we really been beefin' with them Calloway niggas all these years!"

The line went silent, and I knew that I had him right where I wanted him. He had two choices—either tell me the truth or keep runnin' from it like he'd been doing all these years. Either way, I'd know what was really up.

"I'll send my men to pick up your brother's body. Stay by the phone," he said and hung up.

"Mothafucka!" I yelled and threw the phone again.

I slowly climbed to my knees, grabbed my bed sheet, and made my way back to Darius' body. I could barely stand to look at his disfigured face. I put the sheet over his face and held him in my arms, stroking his dreads.

"I'm so mothafuckin' sorry," I said as my tears dripped onto the sheet. "The shit that I did was fucked up. I never should've left you. I never should've did that shit. I knew what was going to happen, and I never should've did it. I'm so sorry, Darius. But don't you worry, okay? I'm gonna make sure those niggas feel my wrath! I'm not gon' rest until I put a bullet in every last one of the mothafuckas that did us wrong!"

I sat there, holding my brother with my head against the wall, waiting. Another hour passed before I saw my father's men standing in front of my door. They pulled Darius's body out of my arms, patted me on the shoulder, and took him away. I sat there in the dark with tears stinging my eyes. There was nobody left but me.

After I decided that I was done sulking, I pulled myself up and went into the bathroom to take a shower. I refused to look at my reflection in the mirror because I knew I'd see my brother's face as a reminder of my selfishness. When I stepped out of the shower, I wrapped my towel around my waist and went back into my room. I knew sleep was the furthest thing from my mind, so I threw on some basketball shorts, socks, and a wife beater and walked into the living room. I flipped on the TV and turned the light on in the kitchen. As soon as the light turned on, all I saw was my brother's blood stains on my floor. I walked over to the sink, put some soap on a sponge, and walked over to scrub Darius's blood off my hardwood floor. Tears glided down the tip of my nose as I scrubbed.

"I'm so sorry," I cried.

I turned my attention to the TV momentarily as I wiped my face with the inside of my shirt.

"Breaking News here on WPLG Local News 10. Divers have just recovered an African-American female's body that washed up on shore down in North Miami Beach. There have been no details on the identification of the female, but police are on the scene and have told us that the body seemed to have been dumped there. Lori Bronson has more."

"Yes, I'm here in North Miami Beach where police officers say they've recovered the body of an African-American female who has not yet been identified. Police say that the victim did not drown, but she sustained a gunshot wound injury to the chest, and that's what killed her. Stick with us on News 10 for more information to come."

I stood to my feet and ran over to the TV. The reporter was standing not too far from where we dumped Shiya's body.

"Shiya," I mumbled.

I rested my hand on my chin. My world seemed to be crashing down at my feet all at once, and I didn't have a soul to turn to. All I could see were flashing blue and red lights and dozens of cops swarming into my home like bees to arrest my ass for killing Shiya. I flopped down on the couch as my body seemed to go numb. It was clear that I was going down for some shit soon. I could feel it coming. Either the Calloways were going to catch me slipping or the police were.

As soon as I closed my eyes, Shiya's face popped into my head. Everything about the way she looked was so vivid. I could see the smile in her eyes. Every part of her face creased up when she smiled or laughed. I loved Shiya from the moment I met her. One thing I knew about Shiya from the very beginning was that she was no saint, but I liked that about her. I liked a woman who could get her hands dirty every now and again. But at the same time, she was a loose cannon. I never knew when she was going to decide that she wanted to flip on me and send somebody to handle me like she'd done with Wolfe and Law. Not a day went by that I didn't think about her, but I didn't know if I felt more remorse or relief.

Shiya didn't officially become my girl until our senior year of high school. Even though I was in school, I wasn't focused on shit that had to do with books or learning. I was only worried about how to get money because I was tired of being broke. Being that Damien was the oldest, my father had already taken him under his wing to show him the rules of the game, and Darius and I were left to focus on getting a so-called education.

The first time I approached Shiya, she hit me with so much attitude it made my head spin. I liked that shit, though. She had a real ghetto girl vibe, and I liked how she knew so much about the game. I never asked her how she knew. I just figured she had an older brother or something.

"So, you tryna be my girl?" I asked her.

"What, nigga?"

"You heard me. When you gon' stop frontin' on a nigga? You know you like me. Shit, you probably even love me," I joked.

"You real funny. You should be a comedian when you grow up."

"Damn," I said, holding my chest. "What you tryna do? Break my heart?"

"Oh, please."

Shiya shooed me away, grabbed her books from her locker, and turned to walk down the hall. I followed behind her and tossed my arm around her. She sucked her teeth and shoved me.

"When are you gon' let this shit go?"

"You know I like that tough girl shit you be tryna put on all the time, but you ain't gotta do that with me."

Shiya pursed her lips and ran her tongue over her teeth. She rolled her eyes and then curved her lips into a smile.

"Shut up."

"See? That's better. So, you gon' answer my question?"

"And what question was that again?"

"You gon' be my girl, Nashiya?"

"Hmm... let me think about it."

"Think about it? What is there to think about?"

"Nothing." She smiled. "I just like to see you sweat."

I grabbed her by her waist and pulled her lips onto mine.

"So, I take that as a yes then."

"Yeah." She giggled.

"Cool. So, I'm about to get out of here. I can meet you after school if you want."

"Wait. Where you goin'?"

"Oh, I'm done for the day."

"Nigga, how you done, and we got three whole periods left in the school day?"

"Shit, a nigga ain't feelin' school today. I'm ready to go home and lay up."

"I wanna go."

"For real? You really wanna skip with me?"

"Yeah, let me just throw these books back in my locker real quick," she said.

I followed Shiya back to her locker, watching her hips sway from side to side. I licked my lips as she looked back to take a quick glance at me.

"Stop lookin' at my ass, nigga! I know it's nice!"

"Why I can't look at it? It's mine now."

"Mmhm. We'll see about that. Don't think because we together now that you gon' get into my panties all fast either."

"Oh, that's where you've got it all wrong, Shiya. I fuck with you.

I know I joke around a lot or whatever, but I really fuck with you. We can go at your pace. I'm not trippin' over no pussy."

Shiya smiled and grabbed my hand. We ran out of the school just as the bell rang, smiling and laughing.

Shiya wasn't lying about making me wait to fuck her, but once we started, she was comin' at a nigga for dick anytime she could. She was my girl for two years, and then she ended up breakin' up with me because she said that the only thing I was worried about was making money. I couldn't lie; the shit was true. After I graduated high school, I started getting into the drug game with Damien. Once the money really started flowing in, the bitches followed. I couldn't lie, I did Shiya real dirty at times, but I was young and dumb. I wasn't worried about feelings if I couldn't make money off it. Yeah, I fucked a bunch of other females, but Shiya was the only one to ever have my heart.

Once I found out she was dating Law, I almost lost it. Although I'd never fully came out and told her about our deep seeded family beef, I knew I had brought up their last names before. I held a grudge against her for a minute, thinking she just did that shit to get back at a nigga because I knew she was petty like that. I thought it was a phase that would fizzle out after a few months, but it didn't. I hit her phone up and few times with no response. When all my efforts went unnoticed, I stopped, changed my number, and tried my best to move the fuck on.

When Shiya and I ran into each out down in South Beach months later, I had just got done seeing this girl I'd been fuckin' on from time to time when my schedule allowed. I told her how good she looked and did my best to make her smile and shit then told her I'd gotten a new number. She told me to put it in her phone, so I did. When she handed me her phone, I saw the big ass rock sitting on her finger, and that's when she told me she was going to marry that nigga. I looked her dead in her eyes and told her plain and simple that I was going to kill him. She brushed it off like I was just puffin' out hot air, but I was serious. I told her I'd do anything to be with her again, and that was on my mother, and I went on about my business.

That shit didn't take too long to sink in because the very next day, she called me and asked me to handle Law's older brother for her. She never gave me too much detail, but then again, I never really gave a fuck. When I told her I'd do anything for her, I meant it because that's what a real nigga was supposed to do.

I flipped to another channel on the TV to pull myself out of the deep thoughts about Shiya. The only thing I could think about next was if the nigga I shot started running his mouth to the police. I made a note that as soon as I gave my brother the proper burial, I would find his ass and make sure that nigga never got a chance to talk to the cops or anyone else again.

* * *

It had been almost two weeks since Raquel and I shared words. I'd reached out to her almost every day since she'd left, but she would always send my shit straight to voicemail. I knew she was down in South Beach at the penthouse with Camille, so I tried not to trip too hard. As much as I missed her, I did my best to occupy my time by taking care of things I needed to take care of.

I was in the kitchen when my phone vibrated in my pocket. I pulled it out to see my lawyer calling. My forehead screwed up like I was squinting my eyes from the sun, as I pressed the accept button.

"Clifton, what's up?"

"Andreas, you got a second?"

"Yeah."

"Are you alone right now?"

"Uh, yeah. What's going on?"

"I have some more information for you about Detective Mason if you're still interested."

"I'm always interested. What you got for me?" I asked.

"From the very beginning you told me to look into him because you felt like he was too involved and too overly concerned with locking you up, right?"

"Yeah." I nodded as I took the phone away from my ear.

I pressed the speakerphone button and put my phone down on the countertop so that I could grab a bottle of water out of the refrigerator.

"Well, you were right. He was so eager to lock you up for the murder of Damien Price because he's related to the Price family. It appears that he is their father's nephew."

I popped my head out of the refrigerator and picked up the phone.

"What the fuck did you just say?"

"Yeah, he's the father's nephew, Law. Damien Price was his first cousin."

"Are you fuckin' kidding me?" I yelled as I squeezed the water bottle so tight the top popped off and water overflowed onto the floor.

"Unfortunately, I'm not, but I do have good news. We can take this information to the judge who handled your case and push to get his badge taken away for this. It's against the law for an officer of the law to have close ties to a victim and pursue who he thinks to be a suspect. He should've never been put on that case from the beginning."

"Yo, Clifton. You're blowing my fuckin' mind right now."

"You just tell me what you want to do, Andreas, and I'll make it happen," he said.

I shook my head.

"Nah, man. You've done more than I could've ever asked you to do. I can take it from here."

Before Clifton even got the chance to try and talk me out of some shit, I hung up the phone. I was mad as fuck. I thought that since my case had been dismissed that the detective would have just gone away, but now that I knew he had ties to my enemy, his ass had to be dealt with, too. I picked up my phone and texted my crew to meet at my house in an hour. I knew with the way the wheels in my brain were turning, I couldn't pull everything off alone or even just with Blaze. I needed all hands on deck.

Once Blaze and four of our other niggas got to the house, we went into my office, and I closed the door.

"What's up?" Blaze asked.

"Yeah, what's goin' on? You ain't called us all to the house in a minute," Reaper told me.

Blaze, Grave, Zero, and Trip all nodded in my direction.

"I know it's been a long time since we've all come together, and you know I don't like callin' y'all niggas off the streets and gettin' in the way of you gettin' money if it wasn't important, but I need all hands on deck for this shit."

"What is it?" Trip asked.

"I just came across some crazy information, and I need y'all to do something for me."

"What is this shit about, Law? What type of information?" Blaze asked.

"My lawyer called me a little while ago. You remember the detective that kept sniffin' around, tryna lock my ass up? He's a fuckin' Price."

"Hold the fuck up. What?" Blaze asked.

"Yeah. He's their first cousin, their father's nephew."

"Oh, nah. Fuck that. What's the plan, nigga? You got a plan?" Blaze asked, standing to his feet.

"Yeah. I do. I knew somethin' was up with this mothafucka all along! Now that I got the proof, I want everybody to be on the lookout for his ass. I'm gon' send a picture to y'all phones, and I want word the minute any of you niggas lay eyes on him. You grab his ass, take him to the warehouse, and wait for my instructions, aight? This shit needs to be as clean as possible, you hear me?" I said.

"Law, I'm all with kidnapping and killing his ass, but I thought you said we weren't killin' any cops," Blaze said.

"He ain't a cop. He's a fuckin' snake in the grass, and I'm about to chop the head off this mothafucka," I told him.

* * *

Raquel

I'd always worn my heart on my skin like a tattoo. And once again, I'd let my heart get the best of me. Love had sucked me dry and left me empty. There was a time where I didn't think I could feel any lower than when Derrick cheated on me, but I was wrong. Losing Law had left a void inside me that was so big I knew no other man would ever be able to fill it. I just couldn't get over the fact that his betrayal had left a hole in my heart the size of a bowling ball.

I closed my teeth around the sour lime and sucked it then tossed the liquor down my throat as I sat at the kitchen island in the penthouse. I hadn't spoken to Law since our blow up a couple weeks prior. I was glad to have the penthouse as my getaway place, but I didn't know how long I actually wanted to stay there or how long I was going to keep ignoring his calls and texts saying *I'm sorry* and the *I love you*. I was tired of accepting Law's roses and ignoring the thorns that came along with them.

"You want another one?" Camille asked me, as she held the bottle of tequila in her hand.

"Hit me," I said, extending my glass toward her.

"How you holdin' up? Still happy to have some space, or are you ready to go crawling back?"

"I'm not crawling back to shit, Camille."

"You know what I mean."

"No, I know what you said," I scoffed.

"Oh, girl. Maybe we need to take a chill pill on the liquor. Tequila is supposed to make your clothes come off, but it clearly makes you angry."

"I'm not angry. I'm just saying."

"It's okay to miss him. Even if you don't say it, I know you do. It's all in your grill."

"All in my grill? Camille, please spare me the nineties and two thousands slang, okay?"

"Fuck what you talkin' about, Raqi. That song by Missy used to be my jam, okay?"

"Whatever," I said as I downed another shot.

"I'm just sayin... If you wanna go back to your man, go back to your man, girl. Ain't nobody gon' knock you for that."

"What man? I'm single as a dollar fuckin' bill, Camille."

"So, wait. Let me get this straight. You went from engaged to one nigga to single to in a relationship and engaged to another nigga to being widowed and now you single again?"

"Pretty much." I shrugged.

"Bitch, are you kidding me? You ain't single. You just stupid!" she joked.

"Fuck you, Camille! Yes, I am single!"

"Girl, I don't care what you say. Law don't strike me as the type of nigga to let you go just like that, so even if you think you single, you ain't!"

"Fine! Don't believe me then."

"Don't worry. I won't." She snickered.

"Whatever. I'm done with this conversation. This liquor got me sleepy anyway, so I'm about to go lay down for a little bit. You gon' be aight?"

"Girl, I'm a grown ass woman, okay? I got this," she told me.

"Fine."

"Goodnight, grumpy pants. I hope your ass wakes up with a better attitude!"

"Night!"

I shooed Camille off, grabbed my phone, and went back into my room. I fell across the bed as my head started to spin.

"Fuckkkkkk," I groaned.

I unlocked my phone and scrolled through all of Law's text messages that I'd neglected to respond to. Being away from him made me miss him, but it also gave me the opportunity to think clearly. I realized that although I loved Law and would do almost anything for him, there would always be hidden things about him, things that I would never know, and he probably would never tell me. I could spend a lifetime trying to peel back all his layers, but I just didn't see the point. Truth was, everybody kept secrets, whether good or bad. I, for one, had too many and was experiencing a system overload.

I decided to blame my actions on the liquor coursing through my veins as I started texting Law.

Raquel: Hey...

CHAPTER SIX
Blaze

I was sitting with Heaven at her apartment after we'd gotten back from her doctor's appointment. I couldn't believe she was already in her second trimester. During her next appointment, they told us that we'd be able to know the sex.

"I hope it's a girl," she said as she flipped through the ultrasound photos in her hand.

"You already know I want a lil' boy, a lil' mini me, you know?"

"She can still be a mini you if it's a girl, Blaze."

"Nah, but you know what I mean. I want my lil' nigga to be fresh like me and shit."

"Okay, so look. You can't call my child a lil' nigga. I don't care if it's a boy or a girl. I don't like that shit."

"That's my baby. I'm gon' call it what I wanna call it," I told her as I rolled my eyes.

Heaven's ass was so damn sensitive. I couldn't even joke with her. Everything I said either made her cry or made her mad. Anytime I didn't come around, she would be blowing up my phone, trying to figure out where I was, who I was with, and what I was doing. She was smothering my ass, and we weren't even together... at least not to me.

"Yeah, we'll see about that shit," she said as she rolled her neck at me.

"Man, whatever, Heaven," I said as I took a pull from the blunt I'd just lit.

I glanced over at her as she turned her back to shield her face from my smoke.

"Oh, shit. My fault. You need me to put this shit out?"

"Nah. It's cool. I'll just be in my room until you finish. Maybe that shit will mellow your ass out."

I ignored her comment and shook my head.

"Nah. I'll go outside," I told her as I hopped off the couch and headed for her balcony.

I closed the door behind me and pulled another hit from the blunt. Heaven was driving my ass fuckin' crazy. I fucked with her, but at the same time, I couldn't help but wish our situation was different. I didn't feel connected to her or the baby growing inside her. I didn't like having a baby with someone that I didn't know, but it was too late. Our baby was coming whether I wanted it to or not.

I turned my attention to the front door when I heard a knock. I put the blunt out and peeped my head inside. Heaven was just sitting on the couch, looking at the door.

"Yo, you don't hear that shit?"

"Shh," she said.

"What I gotta be quiet for? Who is it? A bill collector or somethin'?" I asked as I walked back into the house.

"Just shut up, Blaze," she whispered.

"Nah. Fuck that. Why don't you wanna answer the door? Who is it? You expectin' company?"

Heaven sighed and walked over to me. She grabbed both of my hands and looked me in the eyes.

"It's my ex, aight?"

"Your ex?" I said, pulling away from her. "What the fuck is your ex doin' showin' up at your apartment, Heaven?"

"He's been hittin' me up a lot lately. I've been ignoring him, and he said he was gonna show up at my place, but I didn't believe him. And now... I know his promises weren't empty."

"Nah, fuck that. We gon' settle this shit right now," I said as I walked around her and opened the door.

I was ready to pop off on whoever it was standing on the other side. I looked the nigga up and down. His skin tone was the same color as mine, but he was two times my size if not more. He had a low Caesar cut and a goatee that wrapped around his mouth.

"Who the fuck are you?" he asked. "And where is Vaeh?"

Heaven stepped in front of me and took over the conversation before I could respond. I could sense the tension between them as I stared at them while they stared at each other. I wasn't about to play fool to a female, whether she was having my kid or not.

"Am I missing something here?" I asked.

The two continued to stare at each other in silence.

"What are you doing here, Trey?" she finally said.

"What do you mean what am I doing here, Vaeh? I live here."

"Nigga, what the fuck?" I asked, looking at both him and Heaven.

"Correction, Trey. Your ass used to live here. You've been gone for six months now, and your ass needs to leave."

He sucked his teeth and nodded.

"Who's this? Your new nigga or somethin'?" he asked, eyeing me.

"Nigga, don't worry about who the fuck I am. She already told you what is was. Now, get the fuck on before I gotta put my mothafuckin' hands on you."

"Trey, just leave! Now!" she yelled.

"Nah. I'm not goin' nowhere until you tell me what's really good. So, the two of you are..."

"We're together," she said, cutting him off.

"Wow... you got another nigga in here playin' daddy to my baby, Vaeh? I knew you were a greasy bitch, but damn."

As soon as I heard those words, I popped right back into the conversation.

"Nigga, your baby? That's my fuckin' baby, nigga."

"Oh, yeah? You a gullible ass nigga if you think she told you the truth. That's all Vaeh do is lie to niggas. Ain't that right, baby? That's what you did to me, right?"

I clenched my jaw as I balled up my fist. It was taking everything in me not to turn her whole apartment upside down and fuck his big ass up.

"Nah, that's where you're wrong, fat boy. She lied to your ass, not me."

He scoffed.

"Oh, I get it. You name callin' like a lil' bitch. Lil' nigga, I'll eat you for a snack."

"Oh, word? How 'bout you eat these nuts, nigga!" I said as I shoved him back out into the hallway.

"Stop! Stop right now!" Heaven yelled.

Her cry for peace fell on deaf ears. I was ready to rip his fat ass to shreds. I lunged at him and pushed him against the wall. He flipped me over and threw me onto the ground. Although he was on top of me, I started landing punches to his face and body. I could hear Heaven screaming in the background, but it sounded so far away.

"Stop! Trey! Get the fuck out of here now before I call the police!" she yelled.

I pushed his fat ass off me and stood up. Before I walked past him, I drew my foot back and kicked him in the stomach.

"Don't let me catch your fat ass around here again, or I'll kill you, nigga," I told him.

As soon as I slammed the door, I turned to walk back to the couch. I felt around in my pocket for my weed and started to pour it out onto her coffee table. The two of us sat in silence as she watched me.

"I'm sorry about all that. Are you hurt? I can get you some ice."

I looked down at my knuckles. They were red and swollen, but I shook my head.

"Nah. I'm good."

"Are you sure?"

"Mmhm," I said as I focused on rolling my next blunt.

"Blaze, look at me. What are you thinkin' about?"

"Nothin'. I told you I'm fuckin' good."

"You lyin'. It's all over your face."

"You wanna know what the fuck I'm thinkin'?"

"Yeah, I do."

"You just fuck with bums, Heaven." I shrugged.

"I do, huh?"

"Yeah."

"So, then what does that make you?"

"Nah, sweetheart. I'm far from a bum, but you already knew that."

"Whatever, boy," she said, brushing my comment off.

"I'm just sayin' you fuck with bitch ass niggas. Ain't nothin' to be ashamed of." I shrugged. "This shit is crazy though."

"What's crazy?"

"All this shit, Heaven. Shit just proves I don't know shit about you. Like, why the fuck wouldn't you tell me you had a whole nigga that used to live here?"

"I'm sorry, Blaze. I should've told you, but I just didn't think it was a big deal. Trey and I broke up six months ago! You heard me say that to his face."

"So, if you broke up six months ago, why the fuck would he think you were carrying his fuckin' baby then, Heaven?"

I watched her gnaw on her bottom lip as she figured out the right lie to tell me.

"Since you seem to be struggling with your answer, let me help you out. You were still fuckin' him weren't you?"

"I was." She nodded.

"When was the last time you fucked that nigga?"

Heaven sighed and shook her head.

"I don't know, maybe a couple weeks or so before I met you at the club."

"Wow," I said, rubbing my chin. "I didn't want my brother to be right about you, but he was."

"What is that supposed to mean?" she asked, getting ready to defend herself.

"You know exactly what that shit means."

"Excuse me? That's what you on? Huh?"

"Let me ask you this. Is that my fuckin' baby in there or his? Because if it ain't mine, then let that other nigga take care of that shit, and I'm out! You won't ever have to see me again."

"What the fuck do you mean is it your baby? We got the fuckin' DNA test, Blaze! You were there! You saw the results the same fuckin' time I did!"

I sighed and grinded my teeth against each other. That DNA test was the only thing keeping me from going ghost on her ass. I felt so played that I couldn't even stand to look at her. I stood to my feet, pulled my keys out of my pocket, and grabbed my blunt.

"Look, I'm about to get out of here."

"Really? Don't you think we should finish this conversation, Blaze?"

"Nah, I said what I had to say and so did you."

Heaven shook her head and repeatedly tapped her foot against the carpet.

"Fine! You wanna go, then go!"

I nodded and walked out of her apartment without even closing the door. As soon as I got in the car, I called Law. Even though I didn't want to hear him say I told you so, I still needed his voice of reason.

"What's up?" he answered.

"Yo, nigga. You busy?"

"Nah. What's up? Somethin' wrong?"

I glanced down at my swollen knuckles as I drove.

"I think you were right about shorty."

"Who? Your girl?"

"Nigga, she ain't my girl. We just doin' what we gotta do for the kid. That's all. But shit, right now I don't even want to do that."

"Why not? What happened?"

"I just had to fuck up a nigga for fuckin' disrespecting me. Her fuckin' ex showed up to her house talkin' big shit like that was his baby and all that. Then she came out and told me she was fuckin' him right before she met me."

Law sighed into the phone. Even though I couldn't see him, I knew he was shaking his head at me.

"I don't know what to tell you, nigga. Sounds like to me that hoe sold your gullible ass a dream and got you caught up. What the fuck I been sayin' this whole time? These bitches see dollar signs when they see rappers or athletes, especially down here in Miami. She saw you, and she saw a come up, and now her little plan is coming apart. My question to you is... how the fuck are you gonna move next?"

"I don't know yet." I shrugged. "I mean, it's not like she lied to me about the nigga. I asked, and she told me everything."

"She told you everything after her ass got caught up. Don't let her off that easy. You lucky she agreed to get that damn DNA test done in the first place."

"Yeah, I know. That was the only thing that saved me from goin' fuckin' Tasmanian Devil on her ass."

"Do you believe everything else she's told you up to this point?"

"I told you I don't know what the fuck to believe right now. That shit caught me all off guard. I ain't leave before tellin' her about herself. Believe that."

"I tried to tell your ass at the very beginning to watch her, but you wanted to act like she was your wifey and shit, so I let it go."

"Nah, nigga. The only thing I'm married to is this fuckin' game, and I'm never divorcing this bitch." I chuckled.

"Well, shit. Ain't nothin' you can do now but keep a close eye on her ass. Do what you gotta do for the kid, but keep it at that if you know she can't be trusted," he told me.

I nodded.

"Yeah, you're right. Thanks. I'll see you in a little while. I'm on my way back to the house."

"I might not be here when you get back. I'm meeting with Raquel tonight."

"Oh, shit. You about to get your girl back and shit?"

"I hope so."

"Good luck, nigga," I said and disconnected the call.

* * *

Raquel

After I hit Law's phone, he kept trying to get me to meet up with him. As much as I didn't feel like it, I missed him, so I agreed. He texted me and told me that he would be at the penthouse to pick me up in thirty minutes, so I hurried up and threw on some clothes.

As soon as I heard a knock on the door, I walked over and opened it. Law was standing there with a small leather duffel bag in his hand.

"What's that?" I asked.

"It's for you."

"What is it?"

"Overnight bag with some clothes in it from the house."

"Overnight bag? Law, where exactly are we going?"

"I just want you to come with me somewhere."

"Somewhere like where?"

"Can you just stop asking questions and come?"

"Nah. You need to tell me where you want me to go with you."

"It's a surprise."

I huffed and shook my head. I didn't have time to argue with him. If he wanted to get me out of the house, I wasn't going to object. I grabbed the bag from Law and followed him out of the penthouse.

"You likin' it over here?" he asked as he pressed the elevator button.

"Yeah. It's cool."

"You enjoying your *space* away from me?"

"Law, shut up because you already know you don't care."

"I do care, baby."

"Don't call me that."

"Damn. I can't call you baby no more?" he asked, holding his chest.

"Nope." I smirked.

When we got to the car, I gazed out of my window. Law pressed the button to start the engine then turned the radio on. I started to nod my head to the music. I could see Law glancing over at me through my peripheral, but he wouldn't say anything.

"Why you keep lookin' at me?" I asked.

"First, I can't call you baby, and now, I can't even look at you? What can I do?"

I shrugged and decided against giving him an answer. The more Law drove, the more my surroundings started to look familiar. We were pulling into Biscayne Bay.

"Wait. Isn't this Alastair's yacht?" I asked.

"Yeah. He uh... loaned it to us for the night."

"Why would he do that?"

"You sure are asking a lot of questions, Raquel." He sighed.

"I'll shut up," I said, tossing my hands up in the air.

"Just come on."

I got out of the car and walked around it to meet Law. He held out his hand, and I took it. He led us to the boat and stepped on. I followed him to the dining room table in the lower half of the boat where I'd first met Alastair. I glanced over at the ice melting in the clear ice bucket. There were two unopened bottles of Moët champagne inside.

"Is all this for me?" I asked.

"Yeah, it is."

"Thank you," I said as I shot him a half smile.

Law walked over and pulled one of the bottles out of the bucket and popped the top. Champagne squirted out of the top and into a champagne flute.

"Here you go."

"Thanks."

"We can get off the boat anytime you want, you know. There's a little island not too far away from here."

"Oh yeah?"

"Yeah, with white sand and everything."

"That sounds nice."

Law sighed and shook his head.

"Are you going to keep being this short with me all night, Raquel?"

"I haven't decided yet." I shrugged.

"I guess that's fair enough, but you know neither of us are leaving this yacht until we talk. And I don't mean this bullshit small talk you've been giving me. I mean really talk."

"So, you're holding me hostage... for a second time."

Law blew air out of his nose and cracked a soft smile.

"You think that shit is funny?"

"I'm just being honest. That's all."

"Well, yeah. I'm holding your ass hostage on this fuckin' yacht until you speak to me and we figure all this shit out."

"What is it that you want to talk about, Law? I thought I made myself clear to you that I was done."

"And I thought I made myself clear to you that you can never be done with me."

"I'm pretty sure I could be if I really put my mind to it."

"When are you gon' stop acting like you don't miss me?"

"I never said I didn't miss you, Law."

"Okay, and I'm not letting you leave me. You can get on a plane and go anywhere in the world, and I will be right behind you, Raquel."

"All that sounds good, Law, but we both know that'll probably never happen."

"Try me," he said.

I sighed and shook my head. There was a small part of me that admired his persistence. There was no doubt in my mind that I still loved him with every bone in my body, but I wasn't going to let him off the hook that easily.

"I have a question for you."

"What?" he asked.

"Now that you've had time to think, I just want to know was losing me worth it? Huh? Would you do it again?"

"You know what? It wasn't. All this pain, not having you around... not knowing if you were ever going to come back. It's been tough on a nigga, Raquel. What do you want me to do?"

"What do you mean what do I want you to do? I've told you time and time again what I want you to do, and I still don't know if you get it."

"I do get it, and that's why I brought you here tonight... to show you."

"How far away is the island from here?" I asked, changing the subject.

"Uh, I'm not quite sure. Maybe fifteen or twenty minutes."

"Let's go."

"You want to go to the island?"

"Yeah. I want to see the white sand."

"Okay. I'll tell the captain. I'll be right back."

I nodded and put the glass up to my lips to take a sip of the champagne. It instantly went to my head. *This nigga thinks he's slick*, I thought to myself. When Law came back, I shook my head at him.

"What?" he asked.

"Nothing."

"He said we'll be there in about ten minutes."

"Okay."

"So, do you want to start talking now or wait?" he asked.

"You are real serious about us talking, huh?"

"More serious than anything in this world."

"So, talk. I'm listening."

Law eyed me closely and then sat beside me. He clasped his hands together and put them in his lap.

"Raquel, I'm sorry..."

I blinked hard. Those weren't the words I thought he was going to lead with. In fact, I never thought I'd hear him apologize as sincerely as he did.

"What are you sorry for?"

"For not trusting you enough to let you in. I—I don't know. I love you, Raquel. I think you know that, but I am still learning how to love you the right way. You opened my eyes to the difference in that shit. I used to think that just saying I loved someone was enough, but you taught me that it's not. This love shit is hard work. It's probably the hardest shit I've ever done, but I'm willing to put it all on the line for you... for us."

"Do you really mean that?"

"I've never meant anything more in my life. Do you forgive me?"

"I do." I nodded.

"Do you still love me?" he asked.

"I never stopped loving you, Law. I don't think I could stop if I tried."

"Good because I love you, too. So... can we try again? Please?"

"Yeah. We can." I nodded.

I smiled and then turned my attention to the captain, who walked into where we were sitting.

"We've docked. You two may get off and spend as much time as you want."

"Thank you," I told him.

"Are you ready to go?" Law asked.

"Yeah. I'm ready."

I slid off my sandals, and Law took off his socks and shoes and rolled up his pant legs. He held out his hand, and I placed mine inside his. The two of us walked off the boat and onto the beautiful, white sand. I looked at the sand all around me and the sun setting behind the trees. The sky was a hazy mix of purple, pink, and blue. The ocean waves were glistening underneath the last bit of sunlight as they crashed into one another.

"This is really beautiful," I said.

"I'm glad you like it," he said as he pulled me to him and wrapped his arms around my waist.

Law kissed the back of my neck and rested his chin in the crevice between my neck and shoulder. I turned around and looked in Law's eyes. There was something different in them. Usually, I'd have to search and draw my own conclusions about how I thought he felt or what he was thinking about, but this time, I didn't have to question what he felt for me. There was no doubt in my mind that he loved me and wanted to spend the rest of his life with me.

In the back of my mind, I still questioned if my decision was the right one and whether I was acting out of sound mind and heart. I found myself going back and forth. Although I loved him, his broken promises still lingered on my mind. It was simple. No matter how hard I tried to fight it, my heart's desire was Law.

"What's wrong?" he asked.

"Can you just promise me one thing, Law?"

"Anything. What is it?"

"Just please don't hurt me like that again, okay?"

"Never again," he said as he lifted my chin and kissed my lips.

I was sure the love Law and I shared for each other would be the death of me, but it was going to be one hell of a way to go.

"You remember the first time we were on that yacht together?" I asked.

"Yeah. You damn near told me your whole life story."

"Shut up. You did the same thing!"

"I know. I told you I liked listening to you talk. I still do."

"That's cute, babe."

"You wanna know a secret?"

"What is it?"

"Ever since you left, I don't know. I haven't been right. Today's probably the first day I've smiled in weeks. Shit, it was like I was having Raquel withdrawals." He chuckled.

"Raquel withdrawals? Really?" I said, shaking my head.

"You know you wanna laugh."

"Shut up!"

A part of me was flattered just off the simple fact that he saw me. In my relationship with Derrick, I did love him, but I never thought he saw me for who I really was. Sometimes, I thought he was only with me for a challenge, just to be the first one to get the goods. But with Law, there was never any challenge. He saw me for who I was the first night we met. I was a timid cat who had no idea about my wild side until he brought it out of me. Everything about Law lit a fire inside me that couldn't be extinguished. If it's one thing loving him taught me, it was that there were no short-cuts to loving someone. You have to go through the good, the bad, the ugly, and the in between.

"C'mon. Let's get back on the boat. It's time to celebrate," he told me as he swooped me up into his arms.

He held me as if I was as light as a feather. Instead of taking me back to where we'd left our shoes, he took us to the stern of the boat where Al had a massage pool with his and her massage chairs. Law had already had two glasses of champagne placed in the cup holders.

"You thought of everything, huh?" I asked.

"Kind of."

"How'd you know we'd have something to celebrate?"

"I didn't. A nigga could only hope for the best." He smiled.

Law sat across from me in the chair and downed his entire

glass of champagne then poured himself some more. I reached back and turned on the vibrating chair to relax.

"Does it feel good?"

"Yeah. It does actually. You should turn yours on."

"Nah, I like watchin' you. Your whole little ass body is shaking."

"It's definitely vibrating my pussy a little bit," I teased.

I threw my leg over the chair and dipped my foot in the pool. I gently swayed it back and forth in the warm water, watching the water ripple, then calm again.

"Do you wanna get in?"

"I could, but I don't have a bathing suit."

"You have your birthday suit," he reminded me.

"Really, Law? You want me to strip down out here?"

"Hell yeah. I do."

"Fine." I shrugged.

As soon as those words left my lips, I knew I'd had one too many glasses of champagne. I was acting reckless, and I didn't even care. I pulled my sundress over my head and let it hit the floor beside me. Then I slowly slid down my panties and flung them at him.

"I'm naked. Are you happy now?"

"Yeah, now let me see you get wet."

I walked down the pool steps and lowered my body into the warm water until it came up to my neck. I teased him by rubbing my nipples under the water and then sliding my hands down the front of my stomach. Law licked his lips as he stood and turned the bottle of champagne up to his lips. I could see his dick standing at attention.

"Come here," I told him.

"No, you come here."

Law extended his hand to me, and I slowly stood up and walked up the pool steps. Water cascaded off my body like a waterfall as he took me into his arms. We walked over to the three beach chairs that were on the other edge of the pool. I laid back in the chair, and Law started to kiss my neck and run his fingertips down my chest. His touch was starting to feel good, and it was turning me on. He leaned in to kiss me, and I held my hand out to stop him.

"Law, wait," I said, having a moment of clarity.

"What's wrong?"

"You wanna do it out here?"

"Yes. I want to fuck you outside on this yacht as the sun goes down with nobody watching," he said as he pulled my lips onto his. "Now, relax."

Law spread my legs and started to kiss and massage my inner thighs. He glanced down at my pussy and flipped his tongue against my pearl.

"Mmm..." I moaned as I licked my lips.

My back arched in pleasure every time his tongue flicked my clit. I held the back of his neck as he ran his soft lips up and down my pussy. I slid down the chair to push my pussy closer to his face.

"Shit," I mumbled as my fingertips ran down his back.

Law's tongue made rings around my clit and then laid flat to vibrate against the slit. I closed my eyes and let my head roll back. I could feel myself nearing my climax, but I didn't want to cum from the head. I wanted to cum from his dick. I gently pulled my body away from him and he looked at me, confused.

"It's your turn." I smirked.

Law got up and sat back in the beach chair beside mine. I pulled his shirt from over his head and ran my hands down his hard chest. He pulled his dick out for me to suck on. I hovered over his lap and looked up at him as I wrapped my lips around the tip of his dick. He let out a loud groan as he ran his hand down my spine.

I sucked on the tip and let the spit drip down the sides. My eyes met his as he bit his bottom lip. The way he looked at me made my pussy wetter by the second. I glided my hands up and down his shaft as I admired it from the tip to the base. Then I ran my tongue up the sides and sucked on the head like a lollipop.

"Spit on that shit, Raquel."

I spit on his dick and sucked on the tip. Law's dick had started to become my favorite popsicle flavor. I opened my mouth wide and pushed as much of his dick into my mouth as I could before it touched the back of my throat.

"Shit," he groaned. "Come get this dick, baby."

We looked each other in the eyes as I stroked his dick. Law pulled me up by my shoulders and slid his tongue in my mouth. I climbed on top of him and held the railing of the boat as I bucked hard against his dick. Law took my breasts into his mouth one by one and sucked on my nipples. I bounced up and down on his dick and looked down as my breasts jumped with every stroke. I stuck my tongue out to lick the salty trail of sweat on his neck as he wrapped my arms behind my back and thrust upward.

"Fuck! Yes! Law, baby! Yes!"

My eyes grew wide as my body jerked forward violently. I was about to cum, and I didn't have control over my own motor skills. I bit my bottom lip so hard I knew my teeth had left imprints.

Without letting his dick slide out, he flipped me over and pushed into me. He rested my ankles on his shoulders as he took long, deep strokes into my pussy. He smacked his sweaty chest against me, sticking us together. The humidity outside had me panting like a dog in heat, but I couldn't stop. I wrapped my hands around his face and pulled him into a kiss.

"I love you so much, baby..." I moaned.

"I love you, too."

Law held the back of my head as his tongue swirled around my mouth. He was fucking me so hard I thought I was going to pass out. All I could do was whimper in pleasure. When Law flipped me over onto my side and entered me from behind, I gasped for air. I lifted my leg so that he could dig into my pussy deeper, and he locked his arm underneath my left leg and wrapped his hand around my throat.

"Yeah. That's it, baby. Cum again for daddy," he said as he smacked my titties.

I let my eyes roll back in my head as I focused on welcoming the orgasm that was surging through my entire body. It was the first time I couldn't scream out in pleasure. All I could do was slam my eyes closed as tears ran out of the sides. I was in euphoric bliss.

* * *

Ian

Raquel and I laid together with bottles of expensive wines with names twelve characters long and half-smoked blunts all around us. I had my baby back, and that was all that mattered. Now that we were starting with a clean slate, I thought it would be time for me to tell her the truth and the rest of my plan, starting with Alastair's death.

"Raquel..."

"Yeah?"

"Al didn't lend us his boat."

"I know."

"You know?"

"This is a multimillion-dollar boat. He loves this thing. I don't see him just lending it out to someone. There has to be a reason behind it."

"There is."

"What is it?"

"I killed him weeks ago."

She sat up on her elbows and looked at me.

"You what?"

"He was moving shady, and I knew he was about to flip on me when all that shit got hot with me being arrested and the cops trying to pin that murder on me."

Raquel sighed and locked her bottom lip underneath her two front teeth.

"I'm not going to ask, because for one, it doesn't change anything now, and two, I just don't want to know. I appreciate you telling me though."

"I just feel like if we movin' in the right direction, you needed to know."

"I agree."

"And I also think you need to know the rest of my plan."

Raquel's eyes widened as she looked at me and waited for me to finish what I'd started.

"At first, I thought all we needed to do was go after Darius and Dallas, you know? But the shit is deeper than that. You know that detective that kept coming after you, trying to get you to testify?"

"Yeah. What about him?"

"He's first fuckin' cousins with those Price niggas."

"He's what?" she yelled.

"So, I put a hit out on his ass. Got all my niggas on the lookout for him, and when I find him, I'm gon' kill him, too."

"Law, this is bigger than street shit. You're talking about killing a member of law enforcement. I'm not trying to tell you what to do, but I'm just saying I don't think it's a good idea. Is there any other way around it?"

"I honestly don't know right now." I exhaled. "All I know is I'm not going to be done until every last one of my enemies is six feet under. Then I'll wash my hands of all this shit."

CHAPTER SEVEN

Raquel

L aw and I had been living in bliss for the past forty-eight hours. And as much as I didn't want the feeling to end, I knew it had to. I was losing my balance trying to walk on eggshells around him, making sure I didn't slip up and say something I wasn't supposed to. It was making me lose my damn mind. I walked into Law's office and saw him sitting on the edge of his desk in deep thought. I sighed and walked over to him. I had to tell him the truth about everything with Dallas, Derrick, and what happened to Shiya. It was time we both stepped onto the dance floor and slow danced with the truth.

"Baby, you busy?" I asked him.

"Nah. What's up?"

"I have something I need to tell you."

"Okay. What is it?" he asked.

"Before I say anything, you have to promise to hear me out from beginning to end."

"Is this shit going to piss me off?" he asked.

"Probably." I nodded. "But it's something you need to hear."

"Aight. Fine. Say what you gotta say to get it off your chest."

"My... my ex, Derrick, came into town."

"Hold up. What?"

"Just let me finish."

"Go ahead." He nodded.

"My ex came into town, and he wanted to see me. I ignored

the thought of even seeing him again at first, but then Camille said that I should show him my glow up and inform him of my new relationship and engagement to you."

"And is that what you did?"

"Well, I met with him for all of five minutes. I showed him my engagement ring, and I told him that I had moved on, that there was no more me and him, and that he needed to move on, too."

"So, you really met with this nigga?"

"Law, listen to what I'm saying. Yes. I met with him but only to tell him that I'd moved on with you. That's it."

"Have you moved on? Really?"

"What do you mean have I moved on? Of course! How could you even ask me some shit like that?"

"I asked you some shit like that because, from what you tellin' me, it don't fuckin' seem like it. If you moved on, what the fuck you meetin' with another nigga for, huh? You can say whatever the fuck you want, talkin' about some you wanted to show him you moved on. You don't show a nigga you've moved on, Raquel. You just fuckin' do it!"

I sighed and shook my head. I knew I should've never said anything, but if I didn't, I would've been just as bad as him.

"I'm sorry, okay? I... I didn't look at it like that."

"Yeah. I fuckin' know you didn't."

"But that's not the end of my story."

Law cut his eyes at me. The look on his face told me that he didn't want to hear any more bad news, but he needed to hear what I was about to tell him loud and clear.

"What else? Did you fuck this nigga?"

"No. I didn't fuck him, Law! What the fuck has gotten into you, asking me shit like that! Are you stupid, nigga? Ain't nobody fucking this pussy but you, aight!"

"All I'm sayin' is you goin' and meetin' with the nigga behind my back, so I just had to put the shit out on the table. Straight like that."

"You know what, Law? Fuck you! I swear if you didn't need to hear what else I had to say right now, I'd be out!"

"Then say what the fuck you gotta say then, Raquel. Stop beatin' around the bush with the shit!"

"The night before our wedding, I went to the store, and Derrick was there."

"So, you saw the nigga for a second time?" he asked, cutting me off.

"Just fuckin' listen! Damn!" I yelled.

"Fine. Go ahead."

"Like I was fuckin' saying! I went to the store, and Derrick was there. I told him that he needed to leave me the fuck alone, and I left. I was putting my bags in the car when a car pulled up beside me in the parking lot and pulled me into their car and sped off. Turns out, it was Dallas."

"Hold the fuck up! What?"

"Please, Law. Just let me finish." I sighed. "Dallas held me at gunpoint and took me to this warehouse. It was... it was him and Shiya there. They were going to... to kill me," I said as a tear slipped down my cheek.

"Raquel—"

"No. Stop. Just let me finish. Dallas had the gun aimed at me, but out of nowhere, he hears a sound. Shiya goes to see what's going on, and she comes back with Derrick. I asked him if he was in on their shit, and he told me that he followed the car when he saw me at the store. Dallas was going to kill both of us, but Shiya said she wanted to kill me. She said that she wasn't going to let me be with you. S—she tried to take the gun from Dallas, and the gun went off."

"Raquel... what happened?"

"He shot her and h—he made Derrick and I help him get rid of her body!" I cried.

"Where's her body now?"

"Somewhere in the middle of the ocean as far as I know."

Law drew back and punched a hole in the door right beside me. I screamed.

"What the fuck, Raquel? Why the fuck are you just telling me this shit now? You don't think this was some shit I should've known?"

"I'm sorry! I wanted to tell you right before our wedding, but all that shit happened, and I thought you were gone. Then we weren't speaking, and now that we are, I just needed to come clean!" I cried.

"Man, fuck! This shit isn't you, Raquel! You wasn't supposed to be wrapped up in none of this shit! You weren't supposed to be like all these other bitches out here! You were supposed to be different!"

"What more do you want me to say, Law? I'm sorry I'm not the angel I was when you first met me! I've got blood on my hands too, so that makes me just as dirty as you, so if you can't love me through this shit, then we don't need to go any further!"

Law stopped and looked at me.

"Were your fingerprints on anything?"

"Huh?"

"Think! Were your fingerprints on anything?"

"I don't know. I... I don't think so."

Tears slipped down my face as I stared into his cloudy eyes.

"What happened to that nigga, Derrick? Your ex?"

"Dallas made him... He made him dump her body. When we got back off the boat, he shot him."

"Did he kill him?"

"He said he didn't."

"He said he didn't? You didn't check?"

"No. He threatened to shoot me, too."

"So... why didn't he?"

"What do you mean?"

"Why'd he shoot him and not you?"

"Because of something I—I told him."

"Stop making me pull this shit out of you, Raquel. What the fuck did you say to him?"

"I told him…"

Before I could finish my sentence, his phone rang.

"Aren't you going to answer that?" I asked. I knew he could see the panic in my eyes.

"Nah. I'm waiting for you. That shit can wait."

He ignored the vibrating phone in his pocket and stared at me until it started ringing again.

"Fuck!" he yelled as he pulled his phone out of his pocket.

"Speak!" he yelled.

* * *

Law

"We got eyes on the detective, Law. What do you want us to do?" Trip asked me.

"Grab his ass, and take him to the spot. Call me as soon as you have him. I'm on my way," I said and hung up.

I looked back at Raquel. She had tears in her eyes.

"Don't think we're finished with this conversation," I said as I brushed past her.

I made my way out of the house and started trying to process everything Raquel told me on my drive over to the warehouse. I'd had those Price niggas and that bitch Shiya try to play me, but I was past all of that. I wasn't accepting anymore disrespect from anybody. If I heard my name in a nigga's mouth, it was going to be hollow tips to their skulls with no questions asked. Sometimes, I got tired of being the level-headed one, always calculating every move and making sure I covered my tracks. All that shit was going out the window, and I was going to make another example out of that detective just like how I'd done with Darius.

Although I wasn't the one to kill Shiya, I was glad she got what she deserved for playing with my heart, my time, and most importantly, my money. I should've known her ass was foul, but that's what I got for not protecting my cards. I let all my thoughts of her fade when I put the car in park. I pulled my gun out of my glove compartment and walked into the warehouse with it cocked.

"Where is he?" I asked to no one in particular.

"He's right over there," Trip answered, pointing to my right.

I walked over to where Detective Shawn Mason was sitting. His wrists and ankles were bound to a chair, a black bandanna was tied over his eyes, and a piece of duct tape sealed his mouth shut. I tapped my gun on the top of his head to get his attention.

"We meet again, Detective."

He didn't mumble, moan, or try to scream. He just sat there. I was sure in his line of work, he'd been trained to deal with hostage situations or even what to do when faced with a gun, so he was playing it cool. I tucked my gun in the back of my pants and ripped the duct tape off his lips.

"Shit!" he yelled as he twisted up his lips in pain.

"Do you know who I am?" I asked.

Detective Mason nodded and blew air out of his nose like he knew what he'd gotten himself into. I pulled up a chair, pulled my gun out of my pants, and sat across from him.

"I didn't take the tape off your mouth for you to be quiet. We need to talk man to man. Now, speak," I growled.

"Calloway," he mumbled.

"So, you do know? Good. Let me ask you this. Do you know why you're here?"

I reached up and pulled the blindfold off his eyes so he could look right at me.

"No, I don't," he said with a little more bass in his voice.

"You see, I came across some valuable information about you a little before my court date, and I sat on that shit once the judge dismissed all that bullshit you tried to pin on me. But just recently, I got another bit of information that I want to holla at you about. You need to put the pieces together for me. Can you do that?"

The detective's eyes glanced up at my face then made their way down to the gun sitting in my lap.

"I ain't tellin' you shit, nigga!" He spat.

The spit that flew off his tongue landed on my shoulder. I looked at it and then looked back at him. Without responding, I drew back and slammed my pistol against his jaw.

"Don't you ever do no mothafuckin' disrespectful shit like that to me ever again. You hear me, nigga?" I roared as I hovered over him.

My chest was heaving in and out, and I'd almost decided against trying to get any type of information out of him, but there was shit I needed to know before I killed his ass. I stepped back and took a seat. Blood was leaking from the side of his face, and he looked to be almost unconscious. Three of his teeth were scattered across the floor, so I kicked them to the side.

"Wake up, nigga! I'm not through with you yet. I'll let you sleep when I kill you," I told him.

He blinked slowly and tried to lift his head that was hanging toward the right side of his neck. With his head still hanging low, he lifted his eyes to look into mine.

"W—what do you want to know?" he stammered.

"What was your connection with Damien Price and his family?"

"I don't know what you're talking about."

111

I adjusted myself in my seat and leaned my head back to crack my neck.

"In case you weren't clear on how this shit is going to go, you're not makin' it out of here alive, so you might as well talk while you have the chance. Unless you'd rather me have all the fun and kill you now."

The detective sighed and shook his head. His bottom lip started to tremble as tears welled up in his eyes.

"He was my cousin."

"So, that's why you were trying so hard to pin that shit on me, huh? To get justice for your family, huh?"

"It's not that simple," he said, shaking his head.

"Then make it simple."

"M—my uncle was blackmailing me. He was blackmailing my entire family because he hated my mother."

"What the fuck you mean he was blackmailing you? For what?"

The detective's head rolled back against the back of the chair, and his eyes started to close again.

"Yo, sit this nigga up," I told Trip. "I'm not finished with his ass yet."

Trip walked over and knocked the detective's head back down, and his eyes opened.

"Please... I can barely talk. I need to go to a hospital," he begged.

I glanced up at Trip, and we both started laughing.

"Yo, you got it. I'm callin' the ambulance right now for you, nigga." Trip chuckled.

"What part of *you ain't gettin' out of here alive* didn't you get? Now, keep fuckin' talkin'!"

"My uncle hated my mother because she left Florida and moved to South Carolina when he was a kid. He never got over that abandonment shit. So, when me, my mother, and my brother moved back down here after my sister died, they tried to make amends, but it just didn't work. I knew he always had it out for me and my brother because we weren't like his kids. We weren't street. We didn't get in trouble like they did."

"What the fuck does any of that shit gotta do with why you tried to pin his fuckin' murder on me, nigga? Get to the point!" I yelled.

"Damien killed my partner, and they pinned it on my brother. My brother is sitting in jail right now for something he didn't do!"

"So, why go so hard once Damien was killed? You should've been happy."

"I was, but they told me that if I pursued you and could dig up anything I could find on you to get you convicted, they would make sure my brother went free."

I sat back and watched the tears fall out of the detective's eyes as I listened to him sniffle. He wasn't shit but a pawn that their father was using to get to me. I sighed as I stood to my feet.

"P—please. You have to believe me. Damien's father is a parasite. He will suck the life out of you before you even know he's latched on. W—while he's out there, no one you love is safe."

I lifted his chin with the tip of my gun so that he could look me in my eyes.

"I want you to remember you deserve this. You deserve to suffer, and that's on my brother, my father, and my whole family," I said as I aimed my gun at his chest and let two bullets eject from the chamber.

The chair flew back, and his dead body laid there still tied up. Detective Mason made it clear that my problem wasn't with him. It was with Dallas's father, who was sitting back, hiding in the grass like the snake he was.

"Call up Reaper, Grave, and Zero to help clean this shit up. I'm going home," I mumbled.

"I'm already on the shit," Trip said as he pulled out his phone.

"Oh, and that's not all. Same way we got this nigga, I want the father now, too."

"Hold up, what?"

"You heard me. Tell them niggas when they get here that I want his ass, too. I'll let my brother know. Call me when it's done," I said as I turned to walk away.

CHAPTER EIGHT
Blaze

Even though I still felt like I couldn't trust Heaven, facts were facts. The baby she was carrying was mine, and I had to keep that at the forefront of my mind. As soon as I knocked on her apartment door, her neighbor from across the hall came out.

"Hey." She smiled.

"Uh, what's up?" I asked without bothering to look her way.

"You lookin' for Vaeh, right?"

"Yeah. What? She ain't home or somethin'?"

"Nah. She home. She just probably ain't home alone."

"Fuck you mean by that?" I asked, looking up at her.

She flashed me a wide smile and then shook her head.

"I'm sorry. I shouldn't have said shit, but I just see you over here a lot now, and I figured you should know. She said you her baby daddy."

"Oh yeah?" I asked.

"Yeah. That's what she's tellin' everybody. But I mean, that's none of my business."

"You right. Ain't none of this shit your business. Now, take your nosy ass back in the house," I told her as I turned around and banged on the door.

A few seconds later, Heaven came to the door holding her chest.

"Blaze, what the fuck are you banging on my door like that

115

for? Like you the damn police or somethin'? You scared the shit out of me!"

"What the fuck took you so long to answer the door, Heaven? Huh? You got that fat nigga laid up in here with you or somethin'?" I yelled.

"What are you talking about? I was back in my room sleep. I didn't hear you knock. Damn! You didn't even tell me you were coming over. Your ass just showed up."

"Why the fuck can't I just pop up? Any other time, you want me over here every second of the day."

I walked through her apartment and checked all the bedrooms, bathrooms, and closets for any trace of a nigga before I made my way back to her in the living room.

"Look, Blaze. I don't know what the fuck you're on tonight, but I think your ass needs to either calm the fuck down or leave."

I walked over and sat on the edge of her couch. My forehead met the palms of my hands as I leaned forward and closed my eyes. I couldn't believe I let her nosy ass neighbor get into my head like that. I was just so ready to catch her ass up in a lie that I started to believe anything.

"I'm sorry about that shit," I mumbled.

"Yeah. Like, what the fuck was all that about?"

"I came over here already on a thousand over the shit that popped off last time, and then your nosy ass neighbor came out talkin' about you probably wasn't in here alone and shit, tryna gas me up, and I took it out on you, and that shit wasn't right."

"It's okay," she said as she came and sat beside me. "It shows me you care."

"No. It's not okay. You ain't deserve that shit, and I do care."

"Ooh! Quick! Give me your hand!"

"What? What is it?"

Heaven rested my hand on her stomach so I could feel the baby kick.

"Did you feel it?"

"No. Not really."

"Just concentrate. It's like a quick little flutter. Close your eyes, and just don't think about anything else," she told me.

I turned toward her and put both hands on her stomach. As soon as my eyes closed, I felt a small flutter and quickly reopened my eyes.

"Shit."

"See? You felt it, didn't you?"

"Yeah, I did," I said, curving my lips into a grin.

"Only a little bit of time left before we know the sex." She smiled as she leaned her head on my shoulder.

I nodded, and we sat in her living room in silence, trying to feel the baby move.

"Blaze..." she said as she looked up at me.

"Yeah?"

"I can't believe I'm even about to tell you this right now."

"Tell me what?"

"I don't know... I—I just wish you could see what I see in you."

"What do you mean?"

"I don't know. Even though you've got your flaws, I just think you're a great guy. I know how all this shit between us happened was crazy, but I'm glad it did. You make me laugh. You... I don't know. I think about you all the time and what our baby is going to look like and how you'll be as a father. I guess I say all of that to say... I think I'm falling in love with you, Blaze."

I sat there, staring at her. A part of me thought I was dreaming when she told me she loved me. I didn't see the shit coming. Everything between us started from what was supposed to be a one-night, maybe two-night stand at best. We weren't supposed to be having a baby or falling in love with each other.

"Blaze? Did you hear what I just said?"

"Yeah. I'm sorry. I... uh..."

"It's okay. You don't have to say it back right now if you don't want to."

"I just don't think now is the time for you to be feeling the way you do for me."

"What do you mean? H—how can you put a timing on feelings? The shit just happens, Blaze!"

"I'm just being honest with you, Heaven."

"Honest? Really? Is that what you're being?" she snapped.

"Yeah! I am! Fuck I gotta lie to you for?"

Heaven sighed as her eyes started to turn glossy.

"We ain't gon' do nothin' but keep runnin' circles around each other, huh?"

"What?"

"You heard me. We ain't never gon' go no damn where, Blaze! Not like this! I'm carrying your baby! Your flesh and blood! I'm not asking for a ring today or tomorrow, but I at least thought we were working toward something. How do you not want to share any type of bond with me besides sex, huh? What kind of shit is that?"

I sighed and shook my head. She wanted me to lie to her and paint her the fairytale love story that we were never going to have. All I wanted to do was be there for my kid when it was born. I couldn't be anything more to Heaven because I didn't trust her. I wasn't going to spend the rest of my life checking behind a female wondering if she was playing me with the next nigga. I just couldn't do it.

"Look, Heaven. I'm goin' through some dark fuckin' shit right now, aight? I got a lot of shit on my plate, and if I gotta run back into the streets to handle some shit, then that's what I'm gonna do. That's my first priority right now."

Heaven stood to her feet and hovered over me.

"Do you hear yourself, nigga? Your first priority is the fuckin' streets, and I'm standing here in front of you with your unborn child inside of me?"

"Why the fuck do you keep sayin' that shit? I know you're pregnant with my kid. Everybody knows you fuckin' pregnant with my kid. Who the fuck are you tryna prove it to? Me or yourself?"

"Are you kidding me right now? I just told you I fuckin' loved you, and you're in my face asking me, *yet again*, if I know the baby is yours or not? We already went through this shit! We got the DNA test done! It's your baby, Blaze, whether you wanna be man enough to accept that shit or not! I mean, what the fuck! Would you be goin' this hard on me if you'd met me at a fuckin' grocery story, nigga? No! It's all because of the fuckin' job I had that you wanna label me and throw me in a box with all the other bitches you're used to, and I'm tired of it! I'm fuckin' sick of this shit!" she yelled and slapped me hard across the face.

I quickly jumped to my feet to get in her face. I held my jaw, trying my best not to blow up on her. We both stood in the middle of her living room floor, giving each other death-like stare downs.

"I'm out, Heaven," I mumbled.

"Blaze, wait... wait. I didn't mean to hit you. Please, don't leave," she said, pulling at the back of my shirt as I grabbed the doorknob.

"Get the fuck off me, Heaven," I told her as I swatted her hands away from me.

"Blaze! Please, don't go. I don't want you to leave like this. I'm sorry!"

I brushed her off and walked out of her apartment. I heard her screaming my name as I walked down the hallway. I didn't even bother to turn around. As far as I was concerned, I was done with her ass for good. When I got to my car, my phone vibrated. Figuring it was her, I ignored the call and turned my phone off. All I wanted to do was punch or shoot something or someone and talking to her on the phone wasn't going to make me feel any better.

It took me a few hours before I returned to the house with a bottle of liquor in my hand. I walked into the kitchen, grabbed a glass, and poured me some when Law walked in.

"Yo, why you ain't been answerin' your phone? I've been callin' you," he said.

I looked up at him and shook my head to let him know I wasn't in the fuckin' mood.

"You remember the detective I put everybody on the lookout for?"

"What about him?" I mumbled as I took a sip of my drink.

"I handled his ass earlier."

I glanced up at Law from over the top of my glass then put it down.

"Anything else I need to know?"

"Yeah. We goin' after Dallas and his father now. He's the one who set all this shit up. I want his head on a fuckin' platter," he said.

"Cheers to that," I said, raising my glass to him.

I turned to walk out and went into the living room to drown my feelings into my glass, when Camille and Raquel stumbled into the house sounding like a bunch of horses. Raquel waved at me, and I nodded back at her.

"C'mon, Camille. Let's get your drunk ass upstairs," she said, locking her arms with her.

"Nah. I'm good. You go on up," she said as she looked at me.

I rolled my eyes at her drunk ass and focused my attention back on the TV.

"No, no, no! Keep your pussy in your panties tonight! Come on!" Raquel told her.

"I'm not wearing any panties," Camille said, trying to whisper.

They both laughed. The louder they laughed, the more annoyed I got.

"Yo, can y'all go somewhere with that shit?" I yelled.

"Sorry, Blaze!" Raquel yelled.

"Yeah, oops!" Camille laughed.

"I'm about to leave your ass to fend for yourself if you don't come on, Camille. If you stay down here, don't be surprised if his ass bites your head off. He doesn't look like he's in the mood tonight."

"I'm in the mood tonight." She giggled.

"Bye!" Raquel said and walked upstairs.

Camille struggled to make her way into the living room as she walked past me to head to the kitchen.

"Yo, watch my fuckin' shoes. And if you knock over my cup, you pourin' me some more liquor."

"Boy, shut up! Ain't nobody worried about your little cup," she mumbled before she turned around to look at me.

"You shut up! Drunk ass!"

I rolled my eyes and pulled my blunt from behind my ear.

"Give me some," she said.

"No. You can't hit my fuckin' blunt! Take your ass upstairs, I'm tryna chill! Damn! You really killin' my fuckin' vibe, Camille, and it's about to piss me the fuck off!"

"Stop playin', Blaze. You know we have a good time together," she said as she ran the tip of her acrylic nail against my chin.

I grabbed her hand and balled up her fist.

"Keep your hands to yourself before you start some shit you can't fuckin' finish."

"Maybe I want to start somethin'. And you know just as well as I do I finish anything I start."

"Look, as much as I could stand to bust a nut right now, you already know I got a lot of shit going on. Not to mention, a nigga got a whole baby on the way."

"I know, and my bad. I didn't know you were in a relationship with her. I'm not tryna be on no side chick shit. I was just trying to have another good time with you if you know what I mean."

"Nah, get shit straight. I ain't in no relationship. I'm a free agent, and I can do whatever it is I wanna fuckin' do."

"Then what's stoppin' you right now?" she said, lifting up her dress so I could see her freshly waxed pussy lips.

"Maybe I just don't wanna fuck you." I shrugged.

"Hmm. Now why do I find that so hard to believe?"

"I don't know. Sounds like a you problem to me."

Camille eyed me closely and then turned on her heels.

"Goodnight, Blaze. Oh, and if you change your mind, you know where to find me."

I watched her hips sway side to side as she slowly walked up the stairs. I found myself licking my lips, and I got even more mad. At the end of the day, she was just a piece of pussy to me. The beauty in our situation was that I knew I was just a piece of dick to her as well. I pulled my phone out of my back pocket and turned it back on then turned my attention back to the TV. As soon as my main screen popped up, my phone vibrated. Heaven was calling me. I sucked my teeth and pressed the ignore button then turned my phone back off. I wasn't fuckin' with nothing she had to say to me. Yeah, she might've loved me, but then she turned around and put her hands on me once I expressed what was really on my chest. I wasn't fuckin' with that shit.

I cut the TV off, grabbed my blunt and glass, and walked upstairs to my room, passing Camille's on the way down the hall. Her door was open, so out of curiosity, I peeked inside. She was standing in front of the mirror, naked, brushing her hair. As much as I wanted to keep walking, my legs were stuck like glue and so were my eyes.

"You like what you see?" she asked as she looked at me through her reflection in the mirror.

"Maybe," I said, lifting my glass to my lips.

"Then *maybe* you should come in here and get a closer look," she said as she walked over to me and pulled me into her room by the collar of my shirt.

"Yo, what the fuck is really up with your freak ass?" I asked as I closed the door behind me.

"I like to fuck, Blaze." She shrugged. "I already told you that. More importantly, I like to fuck *you*."

I couldn't lie. I liked fuckin' her too. Her inhibitions didn't exist, and she didn't have a limit on how far she would go to please a nigga. I sat on the edge of the bed, and she bent over in front of me to touch her toes. I watched her ass cheeks spread open a little bit so that I could see the slit in her pussy. I licked my fingers and ran them against her soft skin. She moaned, and I smacked her ass. I stood up, and she pulled my jeans and boxers down around my ankles. I grabbed her breasts and took turns sucking on both her hard ass nipples.

"Mmm. Now you're gettin' to it. It's about time you stopped actin' all scared."

"Shut the fuck up. Ain't nobody scared," I told her.

"Okay. Prove it then."

I sat back down, spread my legs, and watched Camille drop down to her knees. She started sucking my dick as I leaned forward and fingered her pussy.

"Mmm..." She moaned on my dick.

She sucked on the tip and spit on it. The spit dripped off my dick and onto her thighs. She grabbed my dick with both hands and started sucking on it real nasty. She had spit and bubbles flying out of her mouth and everything.

"Damn. Looks like you missed this shit, huh?"

"Hell yeah, I missed it," she said with a string of spit hanging from her lip to my dick.

She rested both of her hands on her knees and started sucking my dick with no hands.

"Mmm. Shit! Just like that. Shit!" I groaned.

I rested my arms back and looked down at her as she slurped my dick. She licked up and down my shaft to get it real nice and wet. I loved the way her lips looked wrapped around my shit.

"It looks like you're ready for me." She smiled as she climbed on top of my lap and eased her pussy onto my dick.

"Shit..." I groaned.

Camille started grinding her hips slowly and then let me thrust my dick into her. I put both of my hands underneath her thighs and pushed her ass up.

"Mmm! Just like that, Blaze," she moaned in my ear.

She leaned to the side and looked back at her reflection in the mirror. She watched her ass bounce up and down. I swear the more she looked back at herself, the wetter her pussy got. It was like she was turning herself on more and more by being her own audience.

I lifted her off my dick, and she crawled onto the middle of the bed. She laid on her back and let her legs spread like butter.

"I heard you're a killer," she saidnas she looked up at me.

"I don't know what you heard, but the only thing I murder is pussy," I said as I pulled her body to the edge, rubbed my dick against her pussy, and then slid back inside her.

"Ooooh, shit," she moaned.

"Shut the fuck up."

"Mmm. Make me." She smirked.

"Shut the fuck up, or I'm takin' the dick away."

Camille chewed on her bottom lip, and I smiled. I grabbed her thigh real tight and pulled her wet pussy deeper onto my dick.

"Oh my God!" she mumbled as she slapped her hand across her mouth.

I pulled my dick out of her and flipped her over so that her ass was up in the air. I spread her ass cheeks to lick her pussy. There was already cum dripping out of it.

"Damn, girl. You creamin' everywhere tonight."

I pushed my dick back inside her, and she spread her ass cheeks so that I could go deeper. She looked back at me as I pressed down on her spine.

"Mmm. Fuck!"

"Shit. It feels like my pussy is about to explode! Keep goin', Blaze! Don't stop!"

I continued to take back shots until I felt myself about to nut.

"Turn around," I said as I quickly pulled out of her.

I latched my hand around the back of her neck as I shot my nut all over her lips and chin.

CHAPTER NINE

Dallas

We had a closed casket funeral for Darius, and I was still sick over that shit. I had so much regret and resentment in my heart that I couldn't even look my father in the eye. I wanted to get to the bottom of what really happened between him and Law's mother, and I knew the only person that would be able to connect me with the truth was Raquel. I had to track her down for two reasons. One, to get her to set up a meeting between me and Law's mother, and two, to see if she knew where I could find her little ex-boyfriend before he pulled the rug out from underneath us all.

Now that Shiya's body had been recovered, I kept checking the news alerts to see if anyone had been able to identify her, but nothing had happened. I was grateful for that. I pulled out my phone to see if I still had Raquel's phone number in it from back when Shiya tried to use me as a distraction between her and Law. I was happy when my thumb landed on her name. Knowing she was probably glued to that nigga Law, I decided against calling her, and texted her instead.

> Dallas: We need to meet.

> Raquel: Who is this?

> Dallas: Let me give you a hint. We share a secret in common.

Raquel: I can't talk right now.

Dallas: That's fine. Tell me where to meet you and I'll be there.

Raquel: I'll let you know.

I locked my phone with hopes that she wasn't trying to play me for a fool. If she was, she was going to have hell to pay.

* * *

Blaze

After a few days of keeping to myself, I decided to return Heaven's phone calls. I pressed her name and then hit the speaker button so that I didn't have to hold the phone. She answered on the first ring.

"Hello?"

"Hey."

"Why haven't you been answering any of my calls these past few days?"

"You know exactly why, Heaven. Don't play dumb."

She exhaled into the receiver.

"Look, Blaze. I know you've read my messages, okay? I've apologized at least 500 times by now. That's all I can do. I can't take it back."

"I know you can't."

"Can you just please come over so that we can talk about this face to face? I don't want to play phone tag with you anymore."

"I'll be over there."

"When?"

"I don't know yet. You got plans?"

"No."

"Okay, so it shouldn't matter when. Just know I'll be over there."

Heaven hung up the phone, and I got up to get in the shower. Once I stepped out of the bathroom and back into my room, Camille was standing there.

"What the fuck are you doing in here, Camille?"

"I just came to see what you were doing."

"I'm about to leave."

"Oh, where you goin'? You want some company?" she asked.

"Nah. I'm going to see my girl."

Her forehead scrunched up so tight she looked like she had a unibrow.

"Hold up. Didn't you just tell me you were a free agent and you 'weren't in a relationship?'" she said, making air quotes.

"I know what I said."

"Wow. You are really something else." She scoffed.

I shrugged her comment off. I thought me lying and telling her I had a girl would send her ass out of my room, but she just sat on the edge of my bed shaking her head.

"Why are you still here?"

"I'm just sitting here trying to figure you out. That's all."

"Figure me out? What the fuck is there to figure out?" I asked.

"Why you're so insecure."

"Insecure? I'm far from that, sweetheart."

"Nah. I'm not tryna be funny. I'm being serious. I may not have no psychology degree, but I've dated enough niggas to know when one is being insecure."

"We never dated

" I corrected her.

"I never said we did. I was just stating facts."

"Facts? I haven't heard one of those come out of your mouth yet."

"Okay. You want some facts? Here they go. You walk around here with all your jewelry on, fuckin' sunshades on at night, always got a bottle of Hennessy in your hands, and some weed on you. You think you the life of the fuckin' party, and just because you slang good dick you think that means a bitch is supposed to bow down to you. Now, all that's cool or whatever, but you wanna know why you do all that shit? You do it as a fuckin' distraction because you don't want the people around you to see how mentally fucked up you are inside. You'd rather portray all the glitz and glamour and shit and never let nobody know the piece of shit you really are on the inside."

"Oh, so I'm a piece of shit now?"

"Yeah, Blaze. You really are."

I knew her guard was down, so I decided to dig in her ass. I used my tongue as a razor to cut into her pride. Wasn't nothing off limits as far as I was concerned. I wasn't the one she needed to be fuckin' with.

"Okay. You want me to keep it a buck with you? Yeah, you wanted this piece of shit to smash, so I did. I smutted your ass out, and you liked every fuckin' minute of that shit. Now, you wanna hang out, and I'm tellin' you I got plans with my girl. So, why the fuck are you still in my room actin' thirsty, tryna play fake doctor?"

"Thirsty? You know what, Blaze? There is something mentally fucking wrong with you! What is it? Huh? What happened to you? Did something happen as a child? You ain't get enough love at home? Nobody put your spelling test on the mothafuckin' fridge? What is it? Because you seriously can't walk around thinkin' that the way you talk to people is okay! Treating women the way you treat them like you got fuckin' mommy issues or something! She lives right behind the house. Go give that bitch a hug or somethin'!"

"Bitch, don't you ever disrespect my mother like that, or I'll smack the shit out of you!"

"You must think I'm afraid to fight a nigga. And if you ever thought you'd get away with putting your mothafuckin' hands on me, you really don't know who the fuck you dealin' with!" she yelled.

"Just get the fuck out of my room, Camille, or I swear to God!"

"You know what? Fuck you, Blaze! I ain't gotta do shit but sit back and watch karma come get your ass!"

Camille stood to her feet and darted out of my room so fast it made my head spin. I was so mad that I knocked everything that sat on top of my dresser onto the floor with one swipe. I hurried up and threw on my clothes and stormed out of the house with my feelings in tow. Although I knew my words had cut Camille deep, she didn't let me go without getting some licks in herself. I couldn't stop replaying her words in my head. I would never admit to her that she was right, even if she hit the nail on the head with some of my actions. It wasn't her place to read me. I pressed my foot all the way down onto the gas pedal and sped off from the house. *And these bitches wonder why my heart is so fuckin' numb*, I thought.

By the time I'd pulled up to Heaven's apartment building, I had calmed down a little. I threw the car in park and got out. When my knuckles collided with her front door, I stepped back. It didn't take her long to shuffle over and open it for me.

"Hey." She smiled.

"Hey."

We stood there, staring at each other for a few seconds in full silence. She stepped up to me and wrapped her arms around my waist.

"I'm sorry."

"Me too," I said as I kissed her forehead.

"So, you wanna come in and talk?"

"Yeah, sure."

Heaven grabbed my hand and led me back to her bedroom where the TV was on. I looked around her room. There was a big cardboard box laying against the wall.

"What's that?"

"A crib. I ordered it from Amazon a few days ago."

"You got it early."

"I'll be twenty weeks soon, Blaze. That's the halfway point."

"Damn. This shit is flying by kind of fast now, huh?"

"Yeah, it is."

"Are you excited?" I asked.

"Sometimes. But I think I'm still more nervous right now, you know? What about you?"

"Definitely nervous."

"Do you have any experience with kids at all?"

"Nah. None whatsoever. You?"

"I've babysat a few times for friends and family, but nothing compares to when you have your own. You can't give that back."

"I know." I nodded.

We both turned our attention to the TV at the same time and watched a commercial. I glanced over at her and caught her staring at me. Her eyes looked wide and sparkly, like if she had been a cartoon character, they would've been googly heart eyes. I knew she wanted to say something, but she didn't, so I asked.

"What?"

"Huh?" she asked.

"Why the fuck you keep lookin' at me like that, Heaven?" I chuckled.

"Lookin' at you like what, boy?"

"You know like what. Like you got somethin' you wanna get off your chest."

"Well, I kinda do."

"What is it?"

"So... I just wanna know... like... where do we go from here?"

"I honestly don't know right now, Heaven. I fuck with you. I really do, but after all that shit popped off with your ex, I just been feelin' like you tryna play me, and it pisses me off every time I think about that shit. Then, on top of that, you throw this baby in my face every chance you get. A nigga is worn out. My life is stressful enough, aight? I just be wanting to get away from that shit when I'm around you, but you don't seem to get that."

"Do you not want the baby anymore?"

I could feel my eyes rolling around in the back of my head. I was so tired of her bringing up the baby. It was ridiculous.

"Heaven, I thought we were past all that. I told you that keeping the baby was your decision, and I was gonna roll with whichever way you wanted to go."

"You're right. You did..." She paused. "I'm sorry. I just want us to get back on the right page. It feels like lately all we do is argue. I just want you to stay... and sleep next to me tonight."

"Are you sure that's all you want?"

"Well, I could go for a nice full-body massage."

"I thought you were going to say you wanted some of this daddy dick?" I chuckled.

Heaven burst out laughing.

"Okay, *Daddy Dick,* who are you? Jodie?"

"Shut up," I said, brushing her off.

"So, you got me with that massage or nah? My back is killing me."

"Strip down, and I got you."

I watched Heaven pull her oversized t-shirt over her head, leaving her wearing nothing but her bra and panties. She was showing, but she was still petite. Her entire body seemed to glow. She crawled back onto the bed and laid on her side.

"You got some baby oil?" I asked.

"Over there on the dresser." She pointed. "Hold up. Let me put a towel down before you get oil all over my damn bed." She laughed.

Heaven walked into the bathroom to get a towel, grabbed the

oil, and came back. She laid on her side and faced the TV, so she could watch it while I rubbed her down.

"Just so you know, I don't know shit about giving a massage for real." I shrugged.

"That's fine. Just do the best you can."

I slid my shoes off and lathered my hands with oil then gently rubbed them into her back. I rubbed my thumbs in circles against her shoulders.

"Oooh, shit. That feels so good."

"Girl, you sound like you gettin' fucked the way you moanin' and shit." I chuckled.

"Hush and keep going. Get my lower back too. That's where it's all knotted up at."

I ran my hands down to her lower back and focused on it like she wanted as she closed her eyes and enjoyed it.

"Blaze?" she mumbled.

"Yeah?"

"You remember how after all that stuff went down at the funeral, and I was trippin' off you running out and doing something crazy?"

"Yeah. What about it?"

"Well, I never told you about my father."

"What about him?" I asked as I massaged the crevices of her shoulders.

"He was killed late one night on his way home from the drugstore when I was seven years old. He was picking up my medicine because I was sick. I'll never forget the sound of my mother's screams when she got the phone call. It still sends shivers down my spine every time I think about it. It's like my personal horror story."

"Damn. I'm sorry to hear that."

"That's the reason why I'm so adamant on keeping you around. I never want my kid to grow up without a father like I had to. The life you live and after what happened to your brother,

Blaze... it just makes me nervous," she said as she rolled over to look at me.

I nodded because I knew exactly how she felt. I'd lost my father, too. I'd neglected to tell her that Law was really alive, but I decided to table that for another time. I didn't want my kid to grow up missing me or worse... not even knowing who the fuck I was. I'd never thought about it like that until I heard her story. I thought back to what Camille said, too. Maybe there was something wrong with me. I'd been so negative because I'd been looking at having a baby as a curse or something negative in my life when it was really something positive. I made a mental note to try and apologize to her for the things I said. I would never want another nigga saying the things I said to Camille to my daughter if I had one.

"Look, Heaven. I don't know what the future holds, but I'm promising you that I'm going to be there for our kid no matter what, and I'm not even gon' be one of those in and out type of niggas or the type of nigga who just gon' throw money at you. I'm gon' really try to be there with you in the trenches and shit, changing diapers and everything."

Heaven giggled.

"And what about late night feedings, doctor's appointments, and birthdays?"

"I'll do everything I can. I promise I'm not gonna fuck this up. I got y'all."

Heaven pulled my body on top of hers, and I made sure not to put all my weight on her. She held the sides of my face in her small hands and kissed me. I hadn't been kissed with that much passion before. I pulled away from her and smiled.

"That's all I could ask for," she told me.

I tugged at her panties, and she lifted her body just enough so I could slide them down. I went back to rubbing the oil down her back and over her ass then spread her cheeks apart so that I could see her juicy pussy. I licked my lips as my dick got hard. I tried to keep my focus on pleasing her without fucking her, so I moved my hands down to her calves and feet.

"Just so you know, I've never rubbed anybody's feet before," I admitted.

"Well, I guess you're just a brand-new man tonight, huh?" She smiled.

She flipped over on her back and I oiled down her breasts, stomach, and the front of her thighs. I massaged her breasts one by one and watched her nipples harden. I rubbed the sides of her pussy without touching it. She spread her legs for me, and I massaged her thighs and the bottom of her ass. I reached my hand down to rub on her pussy as I squeezed her nipple. As soon as my middle finger dipped into Heaven's sweet spot, her body jerked forward.

"Oooh, Blaze," she said, curving her mouth into an "O" shape.

"You like that?"

"Mmhm."

Her body looked so good oiled up. I wanted to taste her, so I had to ask.

"You gon' let me taste that juicy pussy tonight?"

"Mmhm."

I instantly dove into her sweet pussy with my tongue and slurped her juices up like I was on death row and she was my last meal.

"Mmm. Shit. Yeah, daddy. Just like that," she moaned.

I continued to tongue fuck her pussy and flick her clit until she was grasping at the bedsheets.

"Shit! Don't stop! Don't you fuckin' stop, Blaze!" She squealed.

I bent down and flicked her pussy faster and faster until I tasted her juices. After she came all over my tongue, she pulled me up from in between her thighs and laid on my chest until she fell asleep. I stared at the ceiling in the web of my thoughts with a hard dick. The more I tried to settle my brain, the more thoughts flooded in. What were we going to name the baby? Who was it going to look like? Would it have the Calloway last name? If she already had a crib at her house, did I have to go out and buy one for mine?

The pregnancy and the fact that I had a tiny human being on the way didn't sink in until that night. I had a lot of shit I needed to get straight and change about myself before my kid arrived. If I was going to show my kid how to be an adult and make wise decisions, I was going to have to start doing it myself first.

I woke up later that night around 2:00 a.m. by a loud crack of thunder rumbling in the clear night sky. That's when I realized I'd fallen asleep with the TV on. I glanced over and looked at Heaven, who was seemingly sound asleep beside me. The glow from the television lit up the entire room, painting a perfect silhouette of her bare back and juicy ass. I licked my lips. I had every intention of blowing her back out hours before, but I let my thoughts get the best of me. I reached over for the remote and flipped off the TV before snuggling close to her and pressing my dick against her ass. She was sleeping so peacefully that I almost decided against waking her up, but my second head had a different agenda. As soon as my body touched hers, she immediately wrapped my arm around her waist.

"Heaven, wake up," I whispered as I nuzzled my chin in the warm crevice of her neck.

When she didn't budge, I started to gently nibble on her ear, which was her sweet spot. I knew that was a sure way to get her up and turned on. Instead of turning around, Heaven reached her hand around my waist and down to the front of my boxer briefs. She slowly ran her fingertips over the imprint of my dick and felt it pulsate against her hand. I smirked. Even if she wasn't fully awake, she was making my dick rise like a snake charmer.

"You're making my dick hard," I whispered in her ear as I licked it.

To my surprise, she began to rustle in her sleep and then mumbled to me, "Come on, Blaze. I need you."

"Oh, you tryna lose some sleep tonight, huh?"

"Maybe I am," she whispered.

"Shh," I whispered, placing my fingertip over her lips.

I spun her around and laid her on her back. Heaven propped up a few pillows behind her and spread her legs wide. She held her stomach with one hand and locked her arm underneath her knee with the other. I slowly pumped into her as she threw her neck back. She reached around and grabbed my ass to push my dick in deeper.

"Deeper, Blaze. Fuck me deeper."

"Are you sure?"

"Mmhm."

Heaven ran her hands down my arms and then rolled me over onto my back so that she could climb on top of me. As soon as my dick entered her, she sucked in air through her teeth and tossed her head back. Her long weave brushed against my legs as she started riding me like her life depended on it. Heaven thrust her pussy forward and against me and started to buck harder and harder as she neared her climax. Every time her nipples bounced in my face, I would glide my tongue against them.

"Yeah, baby. Suck on them," she said, throwing her head back. "Mmm, shit! Shit!"

"Mmm, yeah. Heaven, cum on daddy's dick," I said as I smacked her ass.

"Yeah, I'm gonna cum! I'm gonna cum!"

I reached over and grabbed the bottle of oil to squirt some down her back and then rubbed it into her skin as she rode me. I held my hands underneath her slippery thighs as I thrust my dick into her. I fucked her so hard my balls slapped the back of her ass.

I switched positions and started fucking her on her side and kneading her nipples between my fingers. She leaned her head back to kiss me.

"Shit. Baby, you feel so good," she moaned, biting her lip.

I thrust into her pussy while gently pulling her hair. Even though she was pregnant and we couldn't do the acrobatics we used to, her pussy still had some power. While I fucked her from the side, I massaged her stomach and breasts as she dug her nails into my knees. I lowered my hand between her thighs and rubbed on her clit. Her body started to jerk and buck against me as she trembled. I knew she was about to cum again, but I wasn't done with her. I let her get her nut then I slipped out of her and pulled her onto all fours.

"Stick that ass in the air, Heaven. I'm not done with you yet."

* * *

Raquel

I walked into Camille's room the next morning and saw her throwing clothes into her suitcase and mumbling to herself. I gently knocked on her door to let her know that she wasn't alone.

"Hey, girl. You okay?"

She turned to look at me with tears in her eyes.

"Raqi, I'm leaving."

"Wait. What? Why? What happened? What's going on?"

"I don't really want to talk about it. Just know that I've thought long and hard about it, and I just feel like it's best that I go back home."

"Okay, but you can't just up and leave without telling me what happened first."

Camille plopped her body down on the edge of the bed as she sighed.

"Blaze and I got into it yesterday, and he said some pretty fucked up shit to me."

"Fucked up shit like what?"

"Saying that he smutted me out, and I deserved it, threatened to put his hands on me, and all that."

"He what?" I yelled. "Where the fuck is he? I'm gonna go say something to his ass right now!"

"Nah," she said, pulling my arm. "I'm good. I need to just head back home and go back to being an adult again. I've been out in Miami so long I should start getting mail here, so it's time for me to go."

I wiped the tear that was about to fall from my bottom eyelid and threw my arms around her.

"But I don't want you to go...."

"I would tell you to come with me, but I already know that's not an option, so I won't say it."

"When does your flight leave?" I asked.

"Tomorrow morning at 10:00 a.m."

"Okay. So that means we have the rest of the day and tonight to have an I'm going to miss you, going away, but you better bring your ass back, farewell party for you." I smiled.

"Bitch, a what?" she giggled.

"You heard me! If tonight is your last night in Miami, we goin' out to paint that bitch red, blue, purple, and all the other colors of the rainbow, too!"

Camille twisted her lips up and then smiled without showing any teeth.

"Fine. As long as there will be alcohol... plenty of alcohol."

"You got it! You know what? Shots for breakfast! Let's go!"

"Wait," she said, pulling my arm. "Where are we going tonight?"

"Hmm. Let's go to Mango's. I've never been there, but I heard it's good for dancing, and I know how much you love to twerk, girl," I said as I locked arms with her and hip bumped her at the same time.

"Mango's sounds good to me. Whatever it is. I'll make sure to have my mangoes sitting upright and perky tonight since it's my last night in the 305!"

"Hell yeah!" I cheered as I spanked her ass.

Camille and I marched down to the kitchen, and she grabbed the liquor while I pulled out my phone. I scrolled through my messages and found the recent thread from Dallas. I felt like shit for texting him, but I knew we needed to talk about Derrick and what we were going to do next.

Raquel: Mango's Tropical Cafe tonight at midnight.

Dallas: Bet.

CHAPTER TEN

Law

"Hey, Raquel!" I yelled, as I walked into the bedroom and looked around.

"I'm in the bathroom."

I turned the knob and walked into the bathroom and saw her standing in the mirror. There was a half empty glass of champagne sitting on the edge of the bath tub.

"Damn, baby. You can't knock? I could've been on the toilet taking a shit or something." She laughed.

"Shut up. Who you gettin' all cute for?"

"I'm trying to get ready to go out, Law. What do you want?" she asked as she pulled her towel tightly across her body and continued to apply her makeup.

I walked over to her and pulled down her towel so that her nipple popped out.

"Where you think you goin'?" I asked.

"I'm going out with Camille."

"And where are y'all goin'?"

"Just out on the town. You know? Girl's time. It's her last night here. She leaves in the morning."

"Girl's time, huh?" I asked.

"Yeah, that's what I said. Now, get out so I can finish getting dressed."

Raquel tried to shoo me out of the bathroom, but I didn't move.

"Why can't I stay and watch you get dressed?"

"You know what? Fine!"

Raquel dropped her towel and started putting on her bra, panties, and jewelry. I loved the way her gold body chain complemented her skin tone. I started stroking my dick through my sweatpants.

"Law, what the fuck are you doing?"

"I wanna remind you what you got at home before you go out and try to find somebody to take my place."

"Are you serious, fool?" She giggled.

"Yeah. Come here."

"No! Stop!"

"I said come here."

"Nope."

I pulled down my sweatpants and walked over to Raquel with my dick in my hand. I pinned her back against the bathroom wall. I made sure I pushed my dick right between her legs so she could feel it.

"Law..." She whimpered.

"What? What I do?" I asked innocently.

"You know what you doing."

"I'm just gon' miss you. That's all. Can a nigga show you how much he gon' miss you?" I asked as I kissed her neck. "Plus, you know the bathroom is our favorite spot."

I pulled her panties down around her ankles, bent her over the sink, and started fucking her from behind.

"Mmm. Shit. Don't stop, baby!"

Raquel propped her foot up on the toilet and arched her back more as I reached around to play with her clit.

"C'mon. Let's go to the room," I told her.

I grabbed her and carried her to the bed. I laid her on her back and kissed her wrists all the way to her elbows, then kissed her soft lips. Her body was my playground. I kissed all the way down her body and on the inside of her thighs then licked her pussy. Her legs trembled at the flick of my tongue.

"Mmm. Spit on my pussy, baby. Get it real wet."

I glanced up at her. She'd never talked dirty like that to me before.

"What you want me to do, Raquel?" I asked, hoping she would say it again.

"I want you to spit on this pussy, baby."

"Mmm," I said as I spit on it and rubbed it in with my thumb. "You know what I want you to do?"

"What?"

"I want you to play with your pussy for daddy. Show me how you pleasure yourself when I'm not around."

Raquel propped her back up against the pillows and spread her legs. She let her fingertips graze her clit as I stroked my dick. Watching her play with her pussy wearing nothing but her bra and that body chain was the sexiest shit I'd ever seen.

"Mmm. It's so wet for you, baby."

She slid a finger inside her pussy and started fucking herself slowly. My dick was throbbing so hard that I could see the veins popping out.

"Mmm, yeah? Show daddy how you cum on those fingers."

The dirtier I talked to her, the faster she finger fucked herself. I sat her breasts on top of her bra to squeeze her nipples and then sucked them one by one.

"Oh shit, Law. You're gonna make me cum!"

"Yeah, baby. Cum all over those fingers so daddy can lick it off."

"Mmm... fuckkkk! I'm about to cum, baby! Ooohhh! Shit! Here it fuckin' comes!" she screamed.

I watched Raquel arch her back as she orgasmed. It was the sexiest thing I'd ever seen in my life.

"Shiiiittt," she said as she collapsed her back against the bed and smacked her pussy.

I didn't waste any time crawling on top of her and pushing my dick in between her walls. Raquel lifted her legs, and I pushed them up toward the ceiling while pushing on her pelvis.

"Mmm. Fuck! Fuck!" she screamed.

I lowered her legs and bent her knees so that her feet laid flat against my chest. She was screaming my name so loud I knew my mother could probably hear us all the way in the guest house. The deeper I went, the more I drove her crazy.

"Shit," I groaned.

"Cum, baby! I want you to cum inside me!" she screamed.

"You want me to cum all inside you?" I asked as I held her waist.

"Mmm. Yesss, baby. Cum in this pussy!"

"This my pussy, Raquel?"

"Yes!"

"Say it!"

"This is your pussy, baby!"

I thrust deep into her one more time and let my juices flow inside her.

"Shit," I said as my body collapsed onto hers and shook.

After I caught my breath, I rolled off her.

"Baby, look at me! You got my sweatin' out my hair and my makeup and shit!"

"So, you tellin' me it wasn't worth it?"

"I didn't say all that." She smiled.

"What's gotten into you tonight?" I asked.

"Too many bubbles in my champagne." She laughed.

* * *

Raquel

I slowly crawled off the bed and yawned. Law had fucked me so good I didn't even want to go out anymore. I just wanted to fall asleep in his arms. I went back into the bathroom and picked my panties up off the ground. Then I made my way over to the sink to fix my hair and reapply my lipstick.

"Shit," I said as I looked down at my left hand.

"What?" he asked.

"I broke a damn nail fuckin' with you!"

"I felt it when you did that shit. You were diggin' your nails into my back so hard I thought you were going to break the skin."

"My bad, babe. It's your fault for coming in here and messing with me in the first place. That's what you get!"

After I finished getting dressed, I popped out of the bathroom and did a quick spin for him.

"How do I look?"

"Naked."

"What?"

"You look naked. You can't wear that shit."

"Babe, it's a crop top and a skirt with some damn heels. You acting like I'm walking outside with a G-string bikini on."

"It doesn't matter what you put on. If you ain't leavin' the house with a full sweat suit and a ski mask on to cover your pretty face, you look naked to me," he joked.

"Boy, shut up." I giggled as I punched him in the shoulder.

Law pulled me into his arms, and I smiled. I was simply lost in the thrill of Law. I closed my eyes and let my entire body fall into his. I felt safest in his arms. Law reached in his pocket and pulled out a wad of cash. He flipped off five, one hundred dollar bills and handed them to me.

"Have a good time, and call me if you need me to pull up."

I kissed his lips and nodded.

"I will, babe."

I tossed my phone and a tube of lipstick into my purse along with the big faces he'd given me and headed down the hallway to get Camille.

"You ready, girl?" I asked as I knocked on her bedroom door.

"Almost. Just let me pull these off. I feel overdressed."

"Pull what off, Camille? All you have on is a dress and no bra."

"These," she said, twirling her panties around her pointer finger.

"Eww, bitch!" I laughed.

Camille flicked her panties at me, and I ducked them.

"Shut up!"

When we got to the club, we stood in the long line and shifted our weight from one leg to the other to aid our aching feet in our heels. As we inched closer to the front, I opened my purse to pull out my ID.

"Shit!" I groaned.

"What? What is it?"

"I don't have my fucking ID!"

"Bitch, you mean we waited in this line the whole time, and you don't have your damn ID?"

"Damn. I'm sorry, girl. Maybe they won't card me when we get up there."

"You better hope they don't because my tits are out, and I'm a nip slip away from becoming partially famous!" She huffed.

I couldn't help but laugh. My snickering quickly ceased when I saw Dallas walking toward us. He stopped when he got to me.

"Step out of the line, pretty ladies. Y'all can roll with me in VIP."

"Nah. It's cool. We good right here," I told him, eyeing him closely.

"Girl, no we not! Excuse me, sir. Thank you. We gladly accept! C'mon, Raqi!"

Without saying anything, I quickly yanked Camille's arm back before she could step out of the line.

"Camille, no. We're fine here. Plus, we're almost at the front."

"Yeah. We're almost at the front, and you don't have your ID with you. I'll be damned if I let my feet ache from standing and not dancing on my last night in Miami!"

I cut my eyes at her and then looked at Dallas who hadn't taken his eyes off me.

"Please, Raqi? For me?" she whined, giving me her puppy dog eyes.

I rolled my eyes and nodded.

"Fine."

Camille led the way as we followed Dallas. I knew all she cared about was having a good time, and I didn't blame her, but I knew Dallas had ulterior motives. He just wanted to keep me where he could find me. Once we got inside, we headed over to Dallas's VIP section.

"Feel free to drink whatever you want on me tonight." He smiled.

Camille headed for the free drinks while I stopped the waitress that was walking by.

"Um, excuse me? How much to buy a table?"

"Five hundred for the basic package," she told me.

"And what does that come with?"

"A bottle of Hennessy or Patrón and two mixers."

I reached into my purse and pulled out the $500 Law had given me and handed it to her.

"Here you go."

"Thanks. I'll get your table sat up right over there." She pointed.

My eyes followed her fingertips, and I saw a table with no one sitting around it.

"Thanks."

I walked over and grabbed Camille by the arm just before she got ready to twerk.

"C'mon."

"Hold up, Raquel. Where are we going?"

"Over there to that table. It's ours."

"Hold up, bitch. You bought us a table?"

"No. I bought you a table. Now, c'mon."

Camille and I walked over to the table and watched all the people swaying their hips to the music. I glanced over and saw Dallas staring at me while sipping his drink. He shot me a quick head nod in the direction of the bathroom and then walked away.

"Hey, uh, Camille. I'm about to run to the bathroom really quick."

"Damn, girl. You breakin' the seal already? You need me to come with you?"

"Nah. I'm good. I'll be right back," I said as I got up and pulled at the hem of my skirt.

I maneuvered my way out of VIP and through the crowd to the back of the club where the bathrooms were. Before I got to even stand in line, Dallas grabbed me by my arm and pushed me into the female bathroom.

"Everybody get the fuck out now!" he yelled.

All the females who were standing in the mirror ran out, and he locked the door behind them. Dallas and I stared at each other in dead silence. I couldn't believe I'd gotten myself entangled in his web, and I had no clue how the fuck I was going to get out.

"You're lookin' real good tonight."

"Cut the bullshit, Dallas. What the fuck do we need to talk about?"

"I bet that pussy taste real sweet under that skirt too." He smirked.

"Let's get some shit straight right now, nigga. If you don't tell me what the fuck you want, you won't live long enough to even dream about tasting my sweet ass pussy again!"

"Here," he said, handing me a burner phone.

"What is this for?"

"Open the messages and read it."

I flipped open the phone and scrolled over to the messages.

"3663 South Miami Avenue... room 3415... What is this?"

"It's the address to the hospital and the room number for where your little boyfriend is staying. You need to go there, and you need to make sure he stays quiet."

"I told you he won't say anything, Dallas."

"I thought the same thing until Shiya's fuckin' body was retrieved out of the fuckin' ocean!"

"Her what?" I asked as my eyes bugged out.

"Exactly. And you're going to make sure he doesn't... by killing him."

"Dallas, no. I can't! Why can't you do it? We've done enough of your dirty work."

"Because this way I'll know our secret dies with both of them. And if you don't do it, it'll die with your ass, too."

I sighed and bit my bottom lip. He had put me in between a rock and a hard place. I knew Derrick had to be dealt with, but I didn't think he needed to be killed. And I for damn sure didn't want to be the one that had to do it. Given that Law knew the situation, I didn't think he'd give me another option. If it was up to him, Derrick would be dead, too.

"Fine. I'll go. But once I go and I do this shit, I'm done. We're done!"

"There's one more thing I'll need from you before I say we're done."

"No, Dallas. That's it! That's fucking it!"

"I want to meet with Law's mother, and you need to set it up."

"You do know Law is back, right? You think he's going to allow you to get close enough to his mother to have a conversation with her? That's never going to happen!"

"You need to fuckin' make it happen," he warned.

"When I tell him, he's going to kill you!"

"You think I'm above killin' your nigga? Huh? I might've failed once, but we'll see each other again. Believe that. I don't give a fuck if we shared a blood relative or not. He's a dead man next time I see him, and that's on my real brothers."

Dallas left the bathroom, and I ran into the stall. My hands were shaking as I put the burner phone in my purse. The last thing I wanted to do was kill Derrick. *Maybe I can just talk to him and see if he remembers anything. For all I know, he could have memory loss after hitting his head like that,* I thought to myself. Tears began to pour out of my eyes like someone had opened the floodgates.

I sniffled as I walked out of the stall and over to the sink to splash a few drops of cold water on my face in hopes to take some of the redness out of my eyes. As much as I didn't feel like it, I had to step out of that bathroom with my head held high, no matter how much I just wanted to grab Camille and run back to the car.

After a few minutes of staring at my reflection and reciting positive affirmations, I reapplied my lipstick and walked out. When I got back to Camille, she was sitting on some Hispanic man's lap.

"Camille, who the fuck is this?"

"Oh, Raqi! I'm glad you're back! This is Esteban. He's agreed to be my hot, Latin lover," she said in her best Sofia Vergara impersonation.

I shook my head and didn't say a word. As much as I wanted to tell her to calm down, it was her last night in Miami, and I wanted her to have a good time. Instead, I sat down and nodded my head to the beat for the next few hours until Camille could barely stand.

"Are you ready to go?" I asked.

"Yeah, girl. I think I'm all salsa, bachata, and twerked out for the night."

"Aight, let's go."

Camille threw her arm around my shoulder, and we walked out of the club to the car. I put Camille in the passenger seat and strapped her in. As soon as I started the car, I could hear her snoring. I flashed my eyes over at her and then down to my purse. I couldn't get Derrick off my mind, and I knew if I sat on the idea of what I had to do any longer, I wouldn't do it at all.

Instead of putting the address to the house in my GPS, I pulled out the burner phone and copied the address. It was a twenty-minute drive, and I knew Camille would sleep through the entire car ride with no interruptions.

When I pulled up to the hospital, I parked the car and left it running, then glanced over at Camille one last time. I made sure the door closed quietly behind me as I looked down to read Derrick's room number.

"Room 3415," I mumbled as I hit the third-floor button in the elevator.

When I approached his room, I looked around at the sparse number of nurses around. I was glad that no one was going to press me about visiting hours being over. My heels clicked against the floor until I opened the door. I took a deep breath and then looked around the corner. Derrick was lying flat on his back with a white piece of tape strapped across his mouth.

"Derrick?" I whispered as I lowered my head on the side of his hospital bed.

He didn't move or respond. I sat my head up and looked over at the dry erase board on the wall. Derrick wasn't asleep; he was in a coma. I could feel tears welling up in the back of my eyes. I didn't even know why I was crying. I was just so mad.

"I told you to stay away. I told you to leave. And now look...

look at what happened. Look at where you are. Ugh! Why the fuck couldn't you have just listened to me!" I sniffled as I looked at him.

I cried over his chest. I didn't feel right killing him when he was already so close to death, but I didn't know what else to do. I sat there, sobbing and stroking his hand until I saw his thumb twitch. I quickly sat my head up and stared at it to see if it would happen again. Another two minutes passed before I saw his thumb twitch again.

"D—Derrick? Oh my God," I said as air flew right out of my lungs.

Derrick groaned as his eyes slowly opened one at a time. It was the first time we'd locked eyes since the night Shiya was killed. I didn't know if I was happy he was alive or devastated that I had to be the one to kill him. He had oxygen tubes propped up underneath his nostrils. I knew I should've called the nurse the minute I saw his thumb twitch, but I didn't. I should've called when he opened his eyes, but I didn't do that either. Instead, I stood up and gently pulled the oxygen tubes from underneath his nose. I could see the panic in his eyes as they started to water. He slowly shook his head.

"I'm sorry, Derrick, but I can't let you leave here," I cried. "I just don't know what you'll say or do."

I watched a tear slip out of Derrick's eye and down the side of his face as he continued to shake his head.

"Shh! Don't cry. I'm so, so sorry, Derrick."

I sat on the edge of his bed and laid my head on his chest. Tears flew out of my eyes as I listened to him struggle to breathe.

"Shh. It'll be over soon," I whispered as I put my hand over his heart. I could feel it slowing down.

There were no words to describe how I felt in that moment. I didn't even feel like myself. It was like I was standing over in the corner, having an out-of-body experience. I hated Dallas, I hated Shiya, and most importantly, I hated myself. When Derrick's heart monitor went flat, I walked over and unplugged it from the wall. I backed out of the room without taking my eyes off him. As soon as the door closed behind me, I turned on my heels and headed down the hall. When I stepped into the elevator, I wiped my eyes with the back of my hand. With the burner phone in my right hand, I texted Dallas.

Raquel: It's done.

As soon as I walked out of the automatic hospital doors, I tossed the phone in the trash can and headed back to my car.

CHAPTER ELEVEN

Raquel

I t was easy for me to get up early the next morning to drop Camille off at the airport because I hadn't fallen asleep. No matter how much I told myself that I really saved Derrick a life of turmoil and looking over his shoulder, I still felt like a monster. I slid on a pair of loose joggers and threw on a t-shirt then headed downstairs to meet Camille at the door. As much as I didn't want to see her go, I knew some shit was about to hit the fan, and I didn't want her anywhere near it.

"Are you sure you're okay, Camille? You really don't have to leave, you know?" I said as I closed the driver's side door.

"Yeah. I'm going to be fine. Are you sure you're okay? You look like a damn zombie, girl."

I nodded slowly.

"Yeah. I'm fine. I was just up all night crying my eyes out because you're leaving me."

"I'm not leaving you! I'm only a phone call and a plane ride away."

"I know, but nothing beats running down the hall and being able to tell you my problems face to face."

"Yeah, I'll miss that, too." She nodded. "But you'll be fine. You've got Law to take care of you. I come a close second only because he's got a dick hanging between his legs."

"Yeah, you're right." I laughed.

"But you two are good now, right?"

"Yeah. We are."

"Good. And I hope you two stay that way. No more lies and secrets and shit because you know that when the love is based on a foundation of secrets, it's sure to crumble sooner than later."

I nodded.

"You're right. I know."

"If you wanna make this shit work, both of y'all are going to have to forgive one another, but you make sure you don't forget, okay?"

I nodded as I whisked my fingertip against my bottom eyelid.

"You'll call me whenever you need me?" she asked.

"Yeah."

"Pinky promise?"

"Promise pinkies." I nodded and wrapped my pinky around hers.

I gave Camille the biggest hug that I could and made sure to squeeze her tight.

"I love you, Raqi."

"I love you more." I waved. "Call me when you land."

She nodded and wheeled her large suitcase into the terminal. I stood and watched her walk until I couldn't see her anymore. Once I got back to the house, I saw Blaze standing in the living room. My face frowned up as I shot him a dirty look. It was his fault my best friend was hopping on a plane to get away from Miami.

"What's your problem?" he asked me.

"You! Why'd you have to say all those things to Camille? You're the reason she left!"

"I know I shouldn't have said all those things to her. I was just in a bad place. I'm trying to be better and do better, aight?"

"Yeah, I hear you, but still. She's my best friend, Blaze. She didn't deserve that."

"I know. And if I ever see her again, I'll tell her myself, but until then, can you just please tell her I'm sorry?"

I rolled my eyes at him when I heard the doorbell ring.

"Can you just let it go and smile for me, please? That's Heaven. She wanted to come over so we could tell everybody the sex of the baby."

"Yeah, sure. Fine," I said, thrusting my shoulder in his direction.

My eyes followed him as he walked over to the door to open it for Nevaeh. She smiled when she saw him. I smiled when she waved at me then sat on the couch to try and hide the sadness I felt for having Camille gone.

"Hey, girl! How are you?" she asked.

"I'm good. Are you excited?"

"I cannot wait to open this damn envelope!" She beamed.

Soon, Law, his mother, Blaze, and Nevaeh joined me in the living room as we all sat around waiting to hear the sex of the baby.

"Law, wow... Hey!" Nevaeh said to him.

"What's up?"

"I didn't believe Blaze when he told me you were back. I told him I wouldn't believe it until I saw it for myself."

"It's me in the flesh. Now, open that shit up."

"Okay, okay! Are you guys ready?" she asked.

"Yeah. Go ahead." His mother smiled.

Nevaeh looked at Blaze and then at all of us.

"It's a girl!" she blurted out.

As much as I didn't want to smile, I couldn't help it. Finding out that Blaze was having a baby girl was the first bit of good news we'd all heard in what seemed like an eternity. Seeing the joy on both Nevaeh and Blaze's faces and seeing how cute she looked being pregnant had me thinking about Law and I making a baby. I knew it would be special. I could see the smile on his face meant that he was genuinely happy for his brother. We all were.

"Are you ready to be an uncle?" I nudged him.

"Yeah. I think Uncle Law sounds good. What you think?"

I giggled. I could see his heart warming up, which in turn

warmed mine as well. It was official. I had baby fever. The happiness only lasted momentarily before Blaze and Law's phones went off simultaneously. Law looked down to check his phone and then glanced up at Blaze. I tried to read their body language since they weren't saying anything. Whatever message they got, they weren't happy about.

* * *

Zero had texted both Blaze and I to tell us he had eyes on Dallas's father. I quickly texted him back to give him the go ahead, and a few minutes later, he let me know that he was en route to the warehouse.

"Raquel, can I talk to you for a minute? In private?"

"Yeah. What's up, baby?"

We walked out of the living room and into the kitchen.

"Look, I gotta head out and handle something."

She looked at me funny and folded her arms across her chest.

"No more secrets, remember?"

"Yeah. I do. Here. Read this," I said, showing her the messages.

"They've got Dallas's father?" she asked as her eyes widened.

"Yeah, and I'm about to handle his ass for all this shit."

"All what shit?" she asked. "You mean the detective stuff or something else?"

"The detective shit, trying to get me to go to jail, shootin' up my wedding, and my fuckin' funeral. That nigga is done disrespecting my family."

"Cutting the head of the snake," she mumbled.

"Exactly." I nodded. "So, I'll be back."

"Wait," she said, holding my arm.

"What?"

"Baby, look at me. Before you go, there's something I need to tell you."

"What is it?"

"I've wanted to tell you this for what seems like an eternity, but it wasn't my secret to tell, but shit is just getting so messy, and I—I just feel like it's time you know the truth."

"The truth about what, Raquel?"

"It's about Damien Price..."

I frowned my eyebrows at her when I heard her mention his name.

"What about him?" I asked.

"Your mother told me something about him."

"My mother? Why would she know anything about Damien?"

"She knows about him because he was her first-born son. He... he was your half-brother, Law. She was with his father before she met your dad."

Her words replayed in my head like a broken record to the point where I didn't even believe it was true. As soon as I opened my mouth to respond, I heard Blaze's voice.

"He's what?" Blaze yelled as he stood in the walkway of the kitchen.

"Shit," Raquel mumbled.

"Bullshit!" Blaze yelled as he walked into the kitchen and slammed his fist down on the countertop. "What the fuck did you just say, Raquel?"

I turned my focus away from my brother and looked back at Raquel. She looked nervous yet relieved at the same time.

"Is it true, Raquel?" I asked.

"Law, I—"

"Is it fuckin' true?" I asked, cutting her off.

"Yes. It's what she told me."

"Nah, fuck this. We gon' figure this shit out right the fuck now," Blaze said.

Raquel trailed behind me as the three of us made our way back into the living room where Heaven and my mother were sitting, looking at the ultrasound photos.

"Ma! Say this shit ain't true!" I yelled.

"What the fuck do you need to tell us?" Blaze yelled at her from behind me.

"Yo, just calm down."

"Nah, fuck that. I need to know what the fuck is really going on?" Blaze yelled.

"What's going on?" she said as she looked at the three of us.

"Raquel let Blaze and I know some very interesting information," I said.

"Yeah, Ma. You need to tell us if that shit is true or not, and you need to say it now," Blaze said.

My mother sighed and then glanced over at Raquel, who immediately put her head down.

"My silver spoon has fed you both and your brother good. I just... all I do is for my kids. That's all any mother can do. I've tried to protect you all for all of these years from my shame, my secrets, and my mistakes," she said, wiping her tears.

"Just say what the fuck you gotta say," Blaze said.

"Just chill, nigga. Give her a minute."

My mother swallowed hard and then looked at Blaze and me.

"The man you murdered... Damien Price. H—he was my first-born son."

"Hold up. What the fuck did you just say?" I asked.

"My father's blood, sweat, and tears went into this shit! And you just gon' disrespect him like that by going to have a baby with his mothafuckin' enemy?" Blaze added.

"Just wait and listen," she said.

"Nah, fuck that," he said, shaking his head.

"I said shut the fuck up and listen, Aston!" she yelled.

Blaze and I stared at her, waiting for any type of explanation that could've made sense out of the bomb she'd just dropped on us.

"I had him before I met your father. Damien's father and I dated when I was younger. I got pregnant, and after I had Damien, he took him from me and left Florida for years. By the time he returned, I'd already married your father and had Asaad," she confessed.

"So, you're really telling me that Damien was our half-brother?" I asked.

I couldn't believe it. The entire time I'd been asking God to protect me from the snakes in the grass, I'd been asking him to protect me from the niggas who were damn near my own family. My blood boiled as I stared at my mother's trembling lips.

"How could you hide this shit from us?" I asked.

"It was a secret I wanted to take to my grave."

"Did Pop know?" Blaze interjected.

"Yes." She nodded with her head hanging low.

"What the fuck, man? It's because of you that Wolfe isn't here right now! If we would've known, my brother would still be alive! Your son would still be alive! At least the only one that fuckin' mattered," Blaze spat.

"Blaze, calm down," Heaven said, trying to grab his arm.

"Nah, fuck that," he said, pulling out his gun.

Heaven screamed and stepped back.

"Blaze, no!" Raquel yelled.

"Shut her the fuck up, Law, or I swear to God I'll put a bullet in her, too!"

"Put the gun down," I said calmly.

"Nah, fuck that. She's the fuckin' reason for all this shit! Our own fuckin' mother, nigga!" he said as he aimed the gun in her direction.

I glanced over at Raquel, who had her trembling hand over her mouth, then over at my mother, who didn't look to be scared at all.

"Blaze, put the mothafuckin' gun down," I told him.

"No, nigga! And who the fuck are you to tell me to do some shit when you couldn't even trust me enough to tell me you faked your death, nigga? Fuck you too!"

I kicked the coffee table out of the way, and Blaze released the safety. I lifted my hands in the air and slowly walked over to step in front of my mother.

"What the fuck are you doing, nigga? Move!"

"Not until you put the gun down."

"Law, I swear to God. Get the fuck out of the way!"

"It's okay, Andreas," my mother said from behind me. "You can move."

My mother gently pushed me to the side as she slowly rose to her feet. She stepped in front of me and looked at Blaze.

"Is this really want you want, son? To take life from the woman who gave it to you? Because if that's what you want to do, then go ahead. Pull the trigger. What else have I got to lose?"

"You're the reason for all of this shit!" he yelled.

"I take full responsibility for my actions, Aston, but killing me is not going to take the pain away. It's not going to change any of the events that occurred. It will not bring your father back. It will not bring your brother back, and it will not bring Damien back either."

"Don't say that nigga's name in my presence! Fuck that nigga, aight? He had everything coming to him! I'd do it again if I could, and I'd make you watch, bitch," he told her through gritted teeth.

"Blaze, look at me," I told him.

"What, Law?" he said, glancing over at me.

"You don't want to do this, man As much as you want to hate her right now, do it. You have every right to. I'm mad at her, too, but this is our mother. We don't get no more. If you do this, that's it. Ain't no reset button on this shit."

"That's where you're wrong, Law. She's not our mother. She was that nigga's mother before she was ours. Now that I know the truth, I don't want shit to do with her."

I slowly walked up to him, and he let me grab his hand. I could tell that deep down he wanted me to stop him. As mad as he was, I knew that he would never be able to forgive himself if he'd taken our mother's life in the heat of the moment. I lowered the gun, took it from him, and put the safety back on. Blaze snatched his hand away from me and then looked at our mother.

"You're dead to me, bitch," he said and walked out.

* * *

Blaze

I'd never been madder at anyone in my life. I never thought I could feel the hate and rage I did toward the woman that gave me life, but I didn't give a fuck about none of that shit. At the end of the day, she lied to her family, and that made her just as bad or as worse as my enemies. I jumped in my car and sped off to the warehouse just as Heaven ran out of the house to try and stop me. I caught a glimpse of her in my rearview mirror and brushed it off. I was too mad to deal with anything that didn't involve taking a life.

Law pulled up to the warehouse right behind me, and we hopped out. I cocked my gun, and he did the same as we walked in without saying a word. I was ready to kill everything moving. When I laid my eyes on Dallas's father, I walked up on him and punched him in the jaw.

"What now, you bitch ass mothafucka? Huh? What the fuck you gon' do now?"

"Blaze, back up," Law told me. "How the fuck you know our mother, nigga?"

My blood started to boil when I saw a smile creep across his face at even the slightest mention of my mother. He spit some blood out of his mouth and looked at Law.

"She used to be my bitch."

"What the fuck you say, mothafucka?" I roared and sent a bullet flying into his kneecap.

"Ahhh, shit!" He groaned as he held his knee.

"C'mon, Law. Just dead this nigga. He ain't gon' tell us nothin'."

"The less you say, the more I'll continue to dig and dig and dig until I come up with the bones of the skeletons that you've tried to bury," Law told him.

"Real niggas take shit to the grave. I ain't tellin' you shit! That's how you keep the longevity in this mothafuckin' game! You think I give a fuck what you do to me? I done lost two sons over this shit! If you gon' shoot me, then shoot me, mothafucka!" he yelled and spit more blood out of his mouth.

"You gon' die anyway, nigga. What the fuck is the point in holdin' onto some shit we already know?"

"I don't give a fuck what you think you know! You'll never know the truth."

"C'mon, Law. Shoot this nigga before I do it myself!" I told my brother.

"Was Damien my mother's son?"

"Damien was my son."

I rolled my eyes and shot a bullet into his other kneecap. He screamed out again in pain, but I didn't give a fuck.

"I do this trigger pullin' shit with no effort. A mothafucka don't even blink anymore. I only fuckin' fear Jesus. Anybody else can catch a bullet, nigga. So you better tell us what the fuck we want to hear!" I yelled.

"I tried to get her back for years, but she was just too wrapped up in your fuckin' father. He wasn't shit but a bitch ass nigga!"

"Go to hell, mothafucka!" I yelled.

"I'll save your mother a place right next to me where she should've been all along."

Law's brows turned up as he raised his arm. He'd finally heard enough talking, and he was ready to put in work. I raised my gun beside him and looked over at him. We both let our guns ring out and emptied our clips into the nigga's body. I watched the smoke seep out and smiled. Dominique Price was dead.

Law and I stared at the dead body before us. I kept pulling my gun although I didn't have anymore bullets left inside. He reached over and lowered my hand and then turned to look at me.

"Why the fuck you ain't tell me you had a problem with me not tellin' you about me fakin' my death and shit?" he asked.

I looked him in his eyes and shook my head.

"I don't know, bruh. I didn't feel no way about that shit at first, but then as time went on, the shit started to eat away at me slowly like you ain't trust a nigga or somethin'."

"Nah, it was never that. You my blood. You know I love you, and I'd do anything for you, but that was just something I had to do on my own to make sure shit worked out the way I needed it to. It was never personal."

"Yeah, I know that now. I know how you move, nigga. The shit just picked at my pride a little. That's all."

"But we good?" he asked.

"Yeah, bruh. We good." I nodded.

163

* * *

Dallas

I'd been calling my father's phone for the past hour, and it kept going to voicemail. I was finally going to let him know that I knew about Damien being my half-brother in hopes that he would come clean. When I couldn't get a hold of him, I decided to call Raquel on the burner phone I'd given her to see if she'd set up the meeting I'd requested between Law's mother and myself. I kept calling her burner phone, and it went straight to voicemail. I thought I'd made myself clear when I told her that we weren't going to be done until I talked to Law's mother. That bitch thought I was playing, so I knew I had to pull up on her ass.

I pulled up and didn't see but one car parked in front of the house, so I decided to take my chances. I cut my lights off and parked on the other side of the road. I put my gun in the back of my pants and held my knife in my hand. I started to creep up to the house when the door opened. I stopped dead in my tracks and watched Raquel walk outside with her flashlight from her phone beaming. She made her way over to her car, and I ran up on her.

"You think you can duck me and I won't pull up on your ass?"

She jumped, and when she turned around, I met her throat with my blade.

"D—Dallas, wait. P— please," she stuttered.

"Shut all that stuttering shit up, bitch. You know why the fuck I'm here. Why the fuck you ain't been answering that fuckin' burner phone I gave you, huh?"

"L—Law is here."

"If he was here, his car would be here, and it's not. Stop fuckin' with me, Raquel. I mean it. I don't want to hurt you, but I fuckin' will. Now take me to my fuckin' answers before I let your ass bleed out in this driveway."

* * *

Raquel

My legs felt like Jell-O underneath me as Dallas held that knife to my throat. I slowly walked forward into the house as he bruised my arm with his grip.

"M—Mrs. Calloway?" I trembled.

"I'm in the kitchen!" she yelled.

I tried to turn my head to look back at Dallas, but he kept my neck straight. We walked into the kitchen, and I made eye contact with her as soon as I could. She glanced at me and then quickly widened her eyes when she realized there was a knife to my throat.

"What the fuck is going on?" she yelled.

"I'm here for answers. Nothing more, nothing less," Dallas told her.

"Answers about what?"

"My father and who the fuck you were to him."

Dallas lowered the knife from my neck, pulled his gun out from behind his back, and placed it on the table. She didn't even flinch.

"Just like your father," she said, shaking her head.

"Look. I came here because you have the answers to the questions I have. My father ain't gon' give 'em to me, so I need you to tell me the fuckin' truth."

Law's mother sighed.

"What makes you think I would tell you anything? And even if I did, why in the fuck would it matter now? Damien is dead!"

"That shit matters to me! I need to know what the fuck is really going on and where this entire beef started from. You're the only one that can tell me that. This is me fuckin' asking you nicely, but I don't have a problem forcing you to tell me what the fuck I want to know," he said, aiming the gun at her.

My eyes widened as she leaned in to the gun in his hand and pressed it into her chest.

"And when you know the truth, what are you going to do about it? You gon' shoot me?"

Instead of pulling the trigger, Dallas pulled his gun back and laid it back on the table.

"That's what I thought. Now, what do you want to know?"

"Everything. Start at the beginning," he told her.

Law's mother sat down at the other end of the table and gestured for him to sit across from her. I stood to the side with my hand clasped tightly around my neck, trying to calm my heartrate and find my phone without being too obvious that I was looking for it. I looked back up at Law's mother when she started talking.

"Okay... I fell in love with you father when I was fifteen years old. We had to keep our relationship a secret because he was almost twenty years old back then. If anybody found out about us, they would've shipped him off to jail without a second thought. Your father took my virginity, and not too long after that, I got pregnant with your brother, Damien. I wanted to name him Dominique after your father, but he didn't want anyone to be able to put two and two together so easily that Damien was his son. He didn't even want the baby at first when I told him, but I kept him. So, by the time I was halfway through my pregnancy with Damien, your father thought of a plan. He told me that after I had our son, he would take him and raise him until I turned eighteen, and then we could be together without him risking jail time. Dom already had his hand in a lot of shit involving the streets, and I didn't want to be the one to send the cops sniffing around his way because of our secret relationship. So, like the young, stupid fool I was, I agreed. I really thought he was going to give me my happily ever after, but I was wrong. The night I gave birth to Damien, I was alone. Your father was too scared to even show up at the hospital. He showed up the next day, brought me a single red rose, and kissed my forehead. By the time the doctor came to check me out the following day, your father had ran off with my son and left me in Miami with nothing."

"So, you wanted to keep Damien?"

"Of course, I did! He was my first child! My flesh and blood! I swore if I ever saw your father again, I'd kill him for what he did to me. Not only did he break my heart, he ripped it out of my chest and stomped on it when he took my baby," she said, wiping tears from her eyes.

"So, what happened when you saw him again? Did you try and take Damien back?"

"I didn't see your brother again until I was twenty years old, Dallas. By that time, Dominique already had your mother raising him as her own, and I'd moved on with my husband. My oldest son was already two years old. As much as I wanted to, I couldn't run back into his life and disrupt it like that. I just couldn't do that to him."

"What about my mother? Did you ever cross paths with her? Did she know who you were?"

167

"Sylvia knew who I was. Everyone who mattered knew what they needed to know."

"Except y'all fuckin' kids. The most important ones, right?"

"I don't think any of us thought it would get this big. At least, I didn't. I can't speak for Dominique."

"Then how did we get to this shit, huh? Because this shit ain't makin' sense to me."

"When your father moved back to Miami, one of the first things he did was track me down. He told me he wanted me back and that he was sorry for leaving me the way he did. I think his excuse was that he was young and stupid, but he'd learned his lesson, and he wanted to show me that he could do right by me. When I told him I was married, and I had another son on the way, he couldn't handle it. He threatened to kill my husband and ruin my family. So, naturally, I told my husband. I thought maybe they would share a few words, and it would be settled, but it wasn't. We buried it, but it just continued to grow and grow until it swallowed all of us up and our children, too. And that's something I can never apologize for enough."

Dallas pushed himself away from the table and stood up. He grabbed his gun and aimed it at her. Time stopped. I just knew Law was going to walk into the house and find both his mother and I dead in the kitchen. All I wanted to do was find my phone, but then I realized I'd dropped it outside when Dallas held his knife to my throat. There was nothing else I could do but stand there with my eyes glued to the two of them. Just when I thought Dallas was going to pull the trigger, he tucked his gun in the back of his jeans, swiped his knife off the table, and turned to leave. My heart was practically leaping out of my chest. Once he was gone, I turned to his mother while trying to slow my heart rate and settle my shaking hands. I looked at her with panic in my eyes, and before I could say anything, she threw up her hand.

"If the Lord decides to take me today or tomorrow, I can go now. My conscience is clean, Raquel."

I nodded without letting a sound pass my lips.

"Raquel..."

"Yeah?"

"I know I've never said this before, but I want to apologize to you for making you keep my secret. I never should've given you my cross to bear. Can you find it in your heart to forgive me?"

"I forgive you."

CHAPTER TWELVE

Raquel

L aw came back the next morning, and I rolled over to see him heading into the bathroom. I immediately jumped up and called his name. He popped his head around the corner and looked at me then his eyes diverted down to the gun lying on top of the comforter.

"What happened?" he asked.

"I kept hearing noises last night, and I guess I just got nervous."

"Do you even know how to handle a gun?"

"No."

"Well, I'm here now, so you don't need to use it. Put it away before you kill both of us," he said as he turned to go back in the bathroom.

"Where have you been?"

"Raquel, you know where I've been."

"Handling Dallas' father?"

"Yes." He nodded.

"Is he dead?"

"Yeah, he's dead."

"So is Derrick... my ex."

Law licked his lips and chewed on his bottom lip as he stared at me, contemplating what to say. He inhaled deeply, cleared his throat, and then spoke.

"Did you kill him, Raquel?"

I sunk my neck into my chest as I nodded.

"Dallas... he..."

"He what?"

I cleared my throat and eased my head into the upward position.

"The night before Camille left... you remember when we went out?"

"Yeah."

"He was there. He gave me a burner phone and told me that Shiya's body had been retrieved from the ocean, and if I didn't make sure Derrick didn't talk, he'd make sure I didn't either. I threatened him with you, and he said he didn't care."

"What the fuck!" he growled. "Why the fuck didn't you call me, huh?"

"I'm sorry, baby. It just all happened so fast! I didn't know what to do! I panicked!"

"You should've called me! You should've let me fuckin' handle it!"

"I know," I said as tears swam out of my eyes. "I'm telling you now because it's done! It's done, okay? It's over."

Law looked at me and shook his head. He looked at me with so much disappointment in his eyes that I almost didn't want to tell him anymore, but I knew I had to keep pushing on. I had to tell him about Dallas showing up at the house.

"That's not all."

"What the fuck else could you possibly tell me, Raquel?"

"Dallas was here."

"He was what! When?"

"Last night! After you and Blaze left, he showed up and held a knife to my throat. He threatened me again, Law. He wanted to meet your mother and talk to her about her relationship with his father."

"This mothafucka was in my house!" he yelled. "Is that why the fuck you had the gun sitting out?"

"Yeah." I nodded. "I'm sorry, baby. I should've told you."

Law spent the rest of the day and into the night making threatening phone calls from his office. He was putting anybody who was somebody in the state of Florida on the lookout for Dallas after he found out that he'd been in the house and talked to his mother. He didn't want him to know that he was coming. He just wanted to get him when he least expected it. A part of me felt like a traitor for finally coming clean about Law's family secret, but they needed to know. I knew they were both sick over the news, but I was glad it was out.

* * *

A Few Days Later...

I walked into the kitchen to grab a bottle of water out of the pantry when my phone vibrated in my back pocket. I pulled it out to see Nevaeh calling me.

"Hello?" I answered.

"Hey, Raquel. I'm sorry to bother you, but is Blaze around? I can't get in touch with him."

"Yeah. He's here. Uh, is everything okay?"

"No. I'm having sharp pains in my stomach, and I don't know what to do. I'm scared."

"Oh my God. Have you called your doctor?"

"I can't get in touch with him. I can't get in touch with anybody. You're the first person who has answered the phone."

"Okay. Hold on real quick. Let me see if I can find him, okay?" I said.

"Okay."

I put the phone down on the kitchen counter and ran down the hall to Law's office and banged on the door.

"Law! Open the door! Is Blaze in there?"

"Nah, he ain't here. He left about thirty minutes ago," he told me as soon as he opened the door.

"Can you try and get him on the phone? It's an emergency.

Nevaeh is having sharp pains in her stomach, and she can't get in touch with anyone."

"Yeah. I'll try and call him."

"Thanks," I said as I rushed back to the phone. "Hello?"

"Yeah, I'm here," she said.

"So, he's not here. Do you need me to come get you? I can take you to the hospital."

"Could you please? I don't want to do this alone. It's so early in my pregnancy. I'm not even in my third trimester yet."

"Okay. Just text me your address, and I'll be on my way. Just please try and stay calm, okay?" I told her and hung up.

As soon as I received the text message with her address, I headed straight to my car. I pulled up to her apartment building twenty minutes later and called to tell her I was outside. A few moments later, I saw her walking toward me, holding the sides of her stomach like she was in labor. I hopped out to open the door for her and she got in.

"Oh my God, Raquel. I swear you're a lifesaver. Like, you don't even know. Thank you so much from coming all the way out here to get me."

"No problem, girl. Have you been able to get in touch with Blaze yet?"

Nevaeh smacked her lips together and shook her head.

"Hell no. Have you?"

"No. Every time I call, his phone goes straight to voicemail."

"Yeah, me too. I've been textin' and callin' him for at least the past hour, if not longer. I don't know what's up with him. I told him to always have his phone on him!"

We both knew exactly why Blaze wasn't answering anybody's calls, but I didn't think it was the time or the place to get into that with Nevaeh. She was already stressed out enough, and I didn't want to add to it. Truth was, I didn't know when Blaze was going to come around and turn his phone back on. He wanted to be as far removed from the real world as possible, and a part of me didn't blame him.

173

"How long have you been feeling like this?" I asked, trying to change the subject.

"A couple days now. It's just like a lot of pressure and some contractions. At first it was bearable, but now it's getting pretty bad. I thought I was just doing too much, so I tried to slow down, hoping I could just give it a few days, but this shit is getting really painful."

"Well, you're doing the right thing. It's better to be safe than sorry. It's probably nothing."

"I hope you're right, but this pain is killin' me, girl."

"So other than the pain, how have you been? How are things with you and Blaze?"

"I don't know. I mean, I think we're doing pretty good. I think it's finally hitting him that our daughter is going to be here sooner than later," she said, glancing down at her stomach.

"Yeah. I really hope he continues to do what he needs to do when it comes to that."

"At first, I wasn't sure about him, you know? But lately, I've just been finding myself thinking about us and how one night brought us together, you know? I mean, that couldn't have just been by chance, right?"

"I know exactly how you feel. It was like that between his brother and I, too."

"How did you two meet?" she asked.

"Uh, we met at a club one night."

"Oh, wow. And look at the two of you now. You've been through so much together. You give me hope, Raquel. You and Law are definitely relationship goals."

"Thank you." I chuckled.

As soon as I pulled up to the emergency room doors, I helped Nevaeh out of my car and the doctors whisked her away to the labor and delivery section to run tests. My head was spinning as I sat in the waiting room, trying to contact Blaze. Every time I tried to talk to a nurse to see what was going on or how Nevaeh was doing, no one would tell me anything because we weren't family.

After three hours of sitting and waiting, I saw a doctor walking down the hall.

"Excuse me!" I jumped up.

"Yes?"

"My sister-in-law has been back there for hours now, and she's pregnant, and no one will tell me anything. I just want to know if she's okay, and if the baby is okay. Her name is Nevaeh."

"I delivered her baby prematurely about thirty minutes ago. She is in the baby NICU and will remain there until her lungs can continue to develop."

"But she was so early. Is the baby going to live?" I asked frantically.

"Your sister-in-law was only a little over twenty weeks along, so it still may be touch and go for the baby for a few more days. We will monitor her around the clock and keep the mother and father updated."

"How is she? How is Nevaeh?"

"She's stable. She is getting some rest right now. You're welcome to pop in and see her but only for a few minutes. She's in room 2121. It's right down the hall."

"Okay. Thank you."

I pulled out my phone to text Blaze that his daughter had been born prematurely then darted down the hallway to her room and walked in. Nevaeh was lying on her back with an IV in her arm.

"Raquel, I didn't think you'd still be here," she mumbled.

"Yeah, I never left. I had to fight like hell to get any information I could on you. Nobody would tell me anything. How are you feeling?"

"Nervous. Have you talked to Blaze?"

I shook my head, and she lowered her eyes.

"I texted him, and let him know that you had the baby. I hope he responds soon."

"Yeah, me too." She nodded. "Did you get a chance to see her?"

"No. As soon as I heard you had her, I came straight down here."

"She's so tiny."

"Yeah. The doctor said she was really premature. Did you and Blaze pick out a name yet?"

"No."

As soon as I opened my mouth to respond, her hospital door flew open. We both turned to see Blaze standing there panting as if he'd run all the way there from wherever he'd been.

CHAPTER 13

Blaze

I hadn't spoken to Heaven or anyone since I stormed out of the house after learning my mother's secret. Even though I'd handled her ex-nigga, I was still mad as fuck at the whole situation. Dallas was still out there, and I wanted to pop a bullet in him just for being that nigga's son. When I finally turned my phone on, hundreds of text messages and voicemails flooded my phone. They were mostly from Heaven and Raquel.

I went to my messages and read Raquel's first since hers was the most recent.

Raquel: Nevaeh had the baby early. Please hurry up and get to the hospital. She's in room 2121 in the labor and delivery unit.

"Man, fuck!" I yelled as I slammed my fist against the steering wheel.

I quickly put the car in drive and sped off to the hospital. When I pulled up, I didn't even bother to find a parking spot. I just pulled the car up by the emergency room door and hopped out. I ran through the halls trying to find the labor and delivery section then found Heaven's room and rushed inside.

"It's so nice of you to show up after your daughter was already fuckin' born," she snapped.

"Heaven..." I said, breathing heavy.

"Save it! You know what, Blaze? Fuck you! I don't want shit to do with you!"

"Heaven, just let me explain!"

"Ain't shit you can say to me that will ever make this shit or ever make me forgive you for missing your daughter's birth! I told you to always stay by your phone! Always!" she said as tears flew out of her eyes.

"You know the shit I've been going through! I got a lot of shit going on in my head right now!"

"You think you the only mothafucka that's going through some shit, Blaze? Huh? I just had our fucking daughter months before she was due! Not weeks! Not days! Months! She's so small she can damn near fit in your fucking hand! Don't tell me you're the only one going through shit! I'm going through shit, too!"

I huffed and stood back. I knew there was no way I was going to win that argument. I didn't even have a good enough excuse. I should've answered her calls. I should've been there.

"All that shit you was talkin' about how you was gon' be there for me and the baby and you had us, and when the shit really fuckin' mattered, your ass was nowhere to be found, Blaze! Nowhere!"

"Heaven, you're right, okay? It's all my fault, and I'm man enough to admit that. I'll do whatever I gotta do to let you know that I'm in this shit with you, aight? I'm sorry. From the bottom of my heart, I am."

"Fuck you, Blaze! Who are you foolin', huh? You don't have a heart! You a selfish, spoiled ass nigga who is still only thinking about himself! You knew all along that I wasn't the one you wanted to be with, right? How much fuckin' longer were you gonna string me along, huh? Until I had the baby? How about you do us both a favor and stop pretending like you're in this shit with me! Stop acting like you love me!"

"What if I'm not?" I asked.

"Oh, please. You said it yourself! We never shared anything but a one-night stand and now a baby. There was never any foundation or anything real between you and I, Blaze! Just face it. We were in over our heads. And guess what? We just fuckin' drowned!"

"Heaven..."

She threw her hand up to silence me and shook her head.

"I'm done with all the shit, Blaze. Get the fuck out! I don't want you around me and I don't want you around my baby!"

"Fuck you mean you don't want me around? You just had my baby!"

"She's my baby! I'm the only one on the goddamn birth certificate because I was the only one that was here!"

After those words fell off her lips, Raquel stepped up from the corner and tried to be the mediator between us.

"Look, y'all. It's gettin' real hot and heavy in here right now, and I think both of y'all are missing the point. You are both parents to a little girl who is down in the NICU fighting for her life right now. Y'all gotta be strong and be there for her, not let your anger get the best of you."

Heaven wiped her eyes and nodded slowly without looking at me.

"I was thinking about naming her Angel."

"I like that name." I nodded. "Can I go see her?"

"Yeah... sure." She nodded.

"C'mon, Blaze. I'll go with you," Raquel told me.

We both walked in silence down to the NICU and stood in front of the big glass. There were so many rules and procedures we had to follow before we could even step foot in there. Raquel and I washed our hands and wiped our cell phones down then put on protective gowns to cover our clothes.

"There she is right there," Raquel whispered as she pointed.

There was my daughter, laying under the lights and hooked up to hundreds of monitors. It was scary seeing her like that, but the fact that she was still alive made me smile harder than I ever had in my life.

"You think she look like me?" I asked.

"Yeah, Blaze. I think she does. Can you believe you have a daughter?"

I shook my head from left to right without taking my eyes off her. I rested my hand on top of the incubator and looked inside.

"There's daddy's baby..."

* * *

Ian

Raquel walked inside the house with the saddest look on her face. She walked over to me and just threw her arms around me.

"What happened? Is everything okay?"

"She had the baby early. Your brother missed it."

"Oh shit. Is the baby okay?"

"Premature. She only weighs two and a half pounds. She's so tiny, Law. She can fit in your hand."

"What did they name her?"

"Angel. She said she wouldn't put his name on the birth certificate since he missed everything. I feel so bad for him. I hope they can work it out. I tried to talk some sense into both of them, but I don't know what's going to happen."

"I told him to watch her fuckin' ass from day one!" I said, shaking my head.

"I hope she comes around. She's just mad right now, and she doesn't want anything to do with him."

I shook my head and flashed her an *I hope you're right* look. I could tell that being around all those babies in the labor and delivery section of the hospital had Raquel's head spinning with baby fever, but it was something we never talked about. It was also something we didn't avoid when we were fucking either.

"Baby," she asked, interrupting my thoughts.

"Yeah?"

"Would you do anything for me?"

"Anything like what?" I asked.

"I don't know. Just anything."

"Where is all this coming from?"

Raquel huffed and shrugged her shoulders.

"I don't know. I've just been thinking about us maybe having a baby."

"I can tell."

"You can? How?"

"That's all you talk about lately."

"No, it's not!"

"Okay. It's not, but you talk about it more than you used to, so I know it's been on your mind."

"So, what do you think about that?"

"Is that something you want?" I asked.

"I think I want to try."

"Try what?"

Raquel looked me in the eyes and said, "I want to have your baby, Law."

CHAPTER FOURTEEN

Blaze

My daughter, Angel Imani Calloway, spent forty-one days in the NICU before she was released to go home. From the moment she came into the word, her health had improved daily, and she didn't show any long-term issues. My baby was a fighter. Although I still hated myself for missing her birth, I promised her from the moment I held her in my arms for the first time that I would never let any harm come her way, and that I would always be by her side.

Heaven ended up coming around after the first week and agreed to put my name on Angel's birth certificate. We were both at the hospital every single day with her, and through that time, we got a lot closer. I never thought I'd be falling for her the way I was, but I couldn't help it. I wanted to do right by her and make the three of us a real family. I was going to ask her to officially become my girlfriend, so we could start looking for our own place together. I wanted Angel to have two parents under the same roof like I did when I was growing up.

When my phone rang, I picked it up to hear Heaven tell me she was pulling up outside. I ran outside and took the baby out of the backseat of Heaven's car when she pulled up to the house. Angel was so beautiful. I couldn't take my eyes off her.

"Here. I'll grab her bag. You just go in the house," I told her.

"No. It's okay, babe. I got it."

Heaven threw the bag over her shoulder and looked inside it. I watched her fish her hand around the bag and then mumble to herself.

"What's wrong?"

"I left her damn formula at my house. Shit!"

"It's fine. I still have some here."

"No. She's on a different kind of formula now, remember? Her doctor changed it last week."

"Shit. That's right. You want me to go out and get some? Just tell me what kind."

"No. It's okay. I'll just run back home and get some. I've got three cans, so I'll bring you one to keep here."

Heaven walked over and handed me the baby bag.

"She's asleep right now, so by the time I get back she'll probably be ready to eat again."

"Okay. You sure you don't want me to go with you? I can run up while you sit in the car."

"Blaze, I got it. It's fine. Go enjoy your time with your daughter."

"What am I gon' do? Watch her sleep?" I asked.

"You do that now anyway," she joked. "But I'll be right back."

I walked over to the passenger side window and tapped on it. She rolled it down and looked at me as she started the engine.

"What's up?"

"I got something to talk to you about when you get back, aight? It's important."

"Is it good important or bad important?"

"Good important," I assured her.

"Good. I'll be back as fast as I can."

Heaven smiled and pulled off. I turned to head back in the house and took the baby upstairs to my room. I took her out of her car seat and laid her on the bed beside me. After flipping through channels and nodding off for a few seconds, I looked at my watch. Heaven had been gone for over an hour. I picked up my phone and dialed her number, but her phone kept going straight to voicemail.

"You've reached the voicemail of Nevaeh Thomas. Please leave a message, and I'll get right back to you. Thanks!"

I hung up before the beep and called her phone three more times. When I got the same response, I texted her, but none of my messages read delivered. I looked over at Angel, who had started to stir in her sleep, and I knew it was only a matter of time before she started yelling at the top of her lungs for food. I scooped her up into my arms and went downstairs and saw Raquel and Law sitting in the living room.

"Hey. Can y'all watch Angel real quick? Heaven left to go back to her apartment and grab some formula, and she ain't back yet. It's been over an hour."

"Maybe she ran into traffic." Raquel shrugged.

"If she was in traffic, she would be answering my calls instead of letting them go to voicemail."

"Hold up. Let me try and call her."

Raquel pulled out her phone and pressed Heaven's name. The phone rang once and went straight to voicemail just like it'd done with mine.

"See? I'm going over there to check on her and see what's up. Can y'all just watch the baby until I get back?"

"Sure." Raquel nodded.

"Thanks. If she wakes up, all her stuff is upstairs in her bag," I said and darted out of the house.

Heaven's phone continued to go to voicemail every time I called her. Police cars and ambulances whizzed by me on the way to her apartment building, but I never paid them any mind until I pulled up behind one. I cut the engine off and got out of the car. I saw Heaven's car pulled up in front of the building with the hazard lights on, so I walked up to it. She wasn't in the car and neither were her keys. I frowned my face up and headed into the building. When I got upstairs to her floor, there were police officers and paramedics running down the hall. Two of them pushed past me and headed straight for Heaven's apartment. I ran up behind them and tried to get in, but they pushed me back.

"Yo, let me in. That's my child's mother!" I yelled.

"Is your child inside sir?" one police officer asked me.

"No. She's back at my house. What the fuck is going on here?"

"Sir, I'm going to need you to step back."

"Fuck that! Somebody tell me what the fuck is going on! Is she okay? Is she in there?"

Before the officer could reply, I glanced inside and saw the paramedics zipping up Heaven's body inside a body bag.

"What the fuck!" I yelled as I pushed past all the police officers until I was inside with her.

I fought my way over to the bag and unzipped it. Heaven was lying in the bag with her eyes open and a bullet wound lodged in her chest. I threw my hands on top of my head as I looked around. Her entire apartment had been trashed. My eyes scanned the area around me and landed on a pool of blood on the living room floor. Her ex, Trey, was lying there with a self-inflicted bullet in his brain.

I could feel the air around me getting thin and my body going numb. I couldn't believe my eyes. I could see the police officers standing around me with their mouths moving, but I couldn't hear a word they were saying. All I heard was ringing in my ears as I stared at the body bag and then back over at her ex. If he hadn't committed suicide, I would've made sure I took his mothafuckin' life myself.

"Sir? Sir! We're going to have to ask you to leave so we can remove the bodies," one officer told me.

He rested his hand on my shoulder, and I looked down at it. It was the first thing I'd felt since I fought my way into her apartment. I knew I needed to move, but I didn't think I could if I tried. I had big plans for Heaven and me. We'd come so far in a short period of time. I actually thought we were going to make it. I'd gone from trying to be in a committed relationship to a single father overnight. All I wanted to do was get back home to my daughter, hold her in my arms, and never let her go.

I slowly turned to walk out of the apartment and locked eyes with her neighbor from across the hall. All she did was shake her head at me as everybody else gawked in silence from their apartments. My feet felt like someone had tied cinderblocks to them, and it was getting harder for my legs to lift them to walk. As soon as I got back in my car, I lost it. I cried so hard no sound came out. I hadn't cried like that since I was a child.

I didn't even know how I made it back to the house in one piece. My eyes couldn't stay clear from all the tears. I'd cried so hard that I'd gotten a migraine. As soon as I opened the front door, I saw Raquel and Law sitting right where I'd left them. Raquel was holding Angel and Law looked right at me. I slowly shuffled over to them and took my daughter into my arms.

"Blaze, I thought you were going to find out what happened to Nevaeh. Where is she? Is she outside?"

I looked up at Raquel and Law with tears in my eyes as I shook my head. I could barely stand to hear the words come out of my mouth.

"She's dead..."

* * *

Law

I looked at my brother as tears slid down his face. I stood up to hug him, and Raquel took the baby from him. It was the first time I'd really seen my brother cry like that since we were kids.

"What the fuck happened?" I asked.

Blaze shook his head, unable to talk. He wouldn't take his eyes off his daughter.

"I don't know if I can do this shit alone, Law. I don't know the first thing about this baby shit," he mumbled.

"Hey. Don't you worry about that shit right now. I got you. We all got you. That's what family is for."

I didn't know how to tell him that I planned to move in on Dallas that night. I knew he wasn't in the right state of mind to even process that shit, so I let it go. If I had to take his ass down on my own, that's what I was going to do. Blaze walked upstairs holding his baby, and I looked at Raquel who was wiping her eyes.

"I can't believe that shit." She trembled.

"I know." I nodded. "But he's going to be aight. We gon' help him as much as we can."

"Yeah." She sniffled. "You're right."

"Raquel, you love me, right?"

"Of course, I do, Law. Why would you ask me that?"

"Because I needed to hear it, and because I'm going after Dallas tonight."

"Law, you can't go after him. Not right now. Not tonight after all this shit."

"I hear you. I really do, but there ain't nothin' you gon' tell me that's going to make me change my mind."

At the end of the day, one more body didn't matter. As long as it wasn't coming from nobody on my team, I didn't give a fuck. I turned to walk back into my office and went into my safe. I heard Raquel's footsteps behind me, and I looked at her out of the corner of my eye.

"Raquel, stop trying to talk me out of going. I already told you my mind is made up."

"I'm not trying to talk you out of it anymore, Law. I'm trying to go with you."

"Go with me? No. Hell no!"

"You can't go alone!"

"Raquel, he's just one man. Let me end this shit man to man with him."

She huffed and folded her arms across her chest.

"Fine."

"Do you trust me?"

"I do. It's him I don't trust."

"Well, that makes two of us."

I put my gun in the holster on my side and kissed Raquel's lips. I could only pray to God that it wouldn't be my last time doing it.

"I'll see you when I get back," I assured her.

I left out of the house and jumped in the passenger seat of Trip's black Excursion. I was tired of playing the cat and mouse game with Dallas. I was going to pull up on him for the last time and settle my beef once and for all. We pulled up outside his high-rise apartment building and waited outside. Trip told me he'd been seeing some girl for a few weeks, and he'd been coming downstairs to let her into the building. We sat outside for an hour until Trip spoke up.

"Yo, ain't that the nigga over there crossing the street?" he asked.

I followed Trip's eyes and saw Dallas jogging across the street wearing a wife beater and a pair of sweatpants. He put his head inside a driver's side window and was talking to someone.

"Yeah. That's that nigga right there. Let's pull up on his ass," I said as I pulled my ski mask down over my face.

Trip threw the truck in gear and sped off down the street. Instead of slowing down when we got close to Dallas, he struck him with his truck. Dallas's body rolled up onto the hood and put a crack in the front windshield. I unhooked my gun from my holster, and as soon as Trip slammed on the brakes, I hopped out and dragged Dallas's body over to the backseat and threw him inside.

"Let's go, nigga! Go!" I yelled.

Trip sped all the way down to the warehouse and threw the truck in park. He helped me pull Dallas out of the backseat and onto the ground.

"Yo, stand out here and keep watch. If I'm not out in fifteen minutes, come get me."

"I got you. Shoot first and don't even ask no mothafuckin' questions," he said as he got back in the truck.

I wrapped his dreads around my hand and dragged him all the way inside. Although he had a few gashes across his face from the truck, he wasn't dead. I was ready to go toe to toe and bullet for bullet with him. He was the last pawn I needed to remove from the board.

"Get the fuck up, nigga. It's time to settle this shit."

Dallas climbed to his feet and threw up his fists.

"You wanna fight me after you hit me with a fuckin' truck, bitch nigga? Fuck that," he said as he dug in his pocket and pulled out a blade.

"You ain't never heard nobody tell you don't bring a knife to a mothafuckin' gun fight, nigga?"

I reached around for my gun and realized I'd left it in the truck when I hopped out to throw Dallas's ass in the back after Trip hit him. Once Dallas realized I didn't have my gun on me, he lunged at me. I grabbed his arm and twisted his wrist so that he would drop the knife. With no weapons on either one of us, we both started going at it, landing blow for blow on one another. Although he'd been wounded, it didn't make him any weaker.

I rushed him and tackled him down to the ground, landing body shots. I could see him reaching for the knife with his right hand, so I drew back and punched him in the eye. Dallas and I continued to roll around on the ground until he grabbed the knife and held it over my chest.

"After everything I've been through, you deserve this shit!" he yelled.

* * *

Raquel

As much as Law didn't want me to go with him, I couldn't just sit at home and wonder if he was going to come back to me or not. I ran upstairs and grabbed the gun from inside the nightstand. I had no idea how to use it or if I was going to have to, but I wanted to make sure my baby had somebody watching his back. I looked out of the window and saw Law jump into a black Excursion. I quickly closed the blinds and ran outside to open his car door. I pressed the button to start the engine and quickly pressed the touchscreen to see the last few addresses in his GPS. I clicked the most recent one and sped off with the gun in the passenger seat.

When I got half a mile away, I shut off my lights and creeped the rest of the way. I was unsure if I was in the right place or not. I saw the black Excursion parked with the lights on, and I shut off the engine at the end of the road. I wrapped both hands around the steering wheel and let out a deep breath. *You got this. Go get your man, girl,* I told myself as I picked up the gun and released the safety.

From that moment on, everything seemed to be going in slow motion. I slowly exited the car and crouched down all the way to the side door. The closer I got to the doorway, the more it felt like I was trapped in a horrible game of hide and seek. I could hear Dallas's voice clearer and clearer, but I couldn't see him or Law.

I looked back at the black truck and crouched down. I quietly peeked around the corner and saw Dallas hovering over Law holding a knife over his chest with both hands. Law held his hands, trying to stop the knife from piercing his skin.

"I'm gonna make your bitch ass suffer just like you did my family! You deserve to rest in hell for what you did, nigga," he spat as he drove the knife toward Law's chest.

My hand shook as I lifted the gun and pulled the trigger. The impact of the gun jolted my arm back, and I dropped it. Dallas fell toward Law, dropping the knife. He pushed Dallas's body off him and looked at the gun beside my feet.

"Did I kill him?" I asked as my hand shook uncontrollably.

Breathing heavily, Law looked over at him and then at me. Dallas rolled over onto his back as his body shook. His chest was rising and falling quicker than his mouth could grasp for air. I knew he didn't have much longer. Law climbed to his feet to get the gun he'd given me and aimed it. Dallas slowly drew in a breath, knowing it would be his last.

"Fuck you," he murmured.

"Nah, nigga. Fuck you!"

Law pulled the trigger, releasing three bullets in Dallas—two in his chest and one in the middle of his forehead. My heart was pulsating out of my chest as I held onto Law. The more I looked at the pool of blood Dallas was lying in, the faster the room started to spin. I quickly held my stomach and fell to my knees. My mouth hit the floor as I threw up everything I had in my system. The floor tasted like copper. Seeing someone die again was my worst nightmare, but having it come to fruition was inevitable.

"Raquel, what the fuck are you doing here?"

"I—I just had to know you were okay," I mumbled.

Law extended his hand to me to pull me up, but I couldn't move. My spine felt like it had metal rods in it and my feet had turned to stone. I was frozen. He tucked his gun away and leaned down to scoop me into his arms.

"It's okay, baby. I've got you."

CHAPTER FIFTEEN

Ian

K illing Dallas was the last piece to my puzzle. And now that he was gone, I could focus on the most important thing to me—my family. I had to make sure my brother had everything he needed to adjust to becoming a single father. I also made sure that he didn't have to worry about planning Nevaeh's funeral or anything. I took care of all that shit. It turns out that her ex-boyfriend broke into her apartment and beat her up real bad then he shot her and shot himself. The police report said that he'd told a few of his friends that he wanted to kill her and the baby, too. It was fucked up that Angel had to grow up without a mother, but I was glad she was getting the chance to grow up at all.

Although shit had been rocky with my mother after her confession, I still made sure she got the care she needed. At the end of the day, she was still my mother, and I couldn't turn my back on her.

I also wanted to focus on making Raquel my wife. Now that there was nothing standing in our way, I was ready to propose again. Although we'd gotten back together, she'd declined to wear my ring again. I wasn't going to be satisfied until she agreed to be my wife. After what she did for me with Dallas, I wanted to pledge the rest of my life to her. I owed her that much.

* * *

Raquel

I walked into the bedroom and stopped dead in my tracks. It was decorated with tealight candles and rose petals everywhere. Jon B's "They Don't Know" was playing softly in the background.

"Law?" I yelled, calling out his name. "Baby, where are you at?"

He popped out from around the bathroom door with a single red rose in his hand.

"Hey." He smiled.

"Hey... What is all this for, baby? What's the special occasion?" I asked as I looked around.

"I ran you a bubble bath, and there's some champagne waiting for you," he said, ignoring my question.

"Okay, but you haven't answered my question."

"I know I haven't. Now, take off your clothes."

"Take off my what?" I asked.

"You heard me. I'm not answering any more of your questions until you do what I say."

I playfully rolled my eyes and unbuttoned my jeans. I pulled them off one leg at a time and then pulled my tank top over my head.

"I smell like baby throw up anyway." I shrugged.

"Even more reason to take your clothes off and get in the tub."

I nodded and pulled off my bra and panties and slowly

submerged my body into the warm water. Law sat on the edge of the bathtub and passed me a glass of champagne.

"Let's toast," he said.

"To what?"

"To us."

"To us." I smiled.

"Raquel, I need to talk to you about something."

"What's up, baby?" I asked as I sat in the bathtub, soaking under thousands of lavender scented bubbles.

"Come here," he said, grabbing my hand.

"Yes?"

"So, I've been thinkin'..."

"About...?"

"I've been thinkin' about spending forever with you," he said.

I turned my neck to look up at him.

"Are you sure you want to try having a wedding again?"

"Third time's the charm. Ain't that what they say?"

I sighed.

"I don't know."

"What is there to know? You love me, don't you?" he asked.

"You know I do."

"Then let's do it. Nobody but you and me."

"You want to elope or something?" I asked.

"I want to do whatever makes you happy. If you want to elope, we'll do that. If you want to have the biggest wedding Miami has ever seen, we can do that too."

I looked at the excitement plastered all over his face, which made me smile.

"Okay. Let's do it! But promise me we'll have a real wedding this time. It doesn't have to have all of the bells and whistles, but I still want it to be nice."

"You can have whatever you want, Raquel. I mean that."

"I'm going to hold you to that, too." I smiled.

"You can hold me to whatever you want as long as you wear

this," he said as he leaned over and pulled my engagement ring out of his pocket.

Law slid my engagement ring back on my finger and pulled my lips onto his.

"I love you."

"I love you, too." I smiled.

CHAPTER SIXTEEN
Raquel

I 'd been feeling sick off and on ever since all that stuff happened with Dallas. I figured that was just something that happened after watching a traumatic event like that. I knew talking to someone I loved would make me feel better, so I picked up the phone to call Camille on FaceTime because I missed her.

"Yo, yo, yo!" she said into the phone.

"Hey!"

"What are you up to?"

"Ugh, just laying around. I'm not feeling too good."

"What's wrong with you?"

"I don't know. I'm just feeling a little sick to my stomach." I shrugged.

"Bitch, are you pregnant?"

"No. I don't know. I don't think so."

"What do you mean you don't think so? You been lettin' Law hit it raw?" she said, chuckling at her rhyming words.

"We've never really used condoms."

"Well, when is your period supposed to come?"

I paused and let my eyes wander around the room while I sat and thought.

"I really don't know."

"Take a test, girl. Do you have one?"

"I think there might be one underneath the sink. I bought a

pack of two a few months ago when I thought I could've been, but it was a false alarm."

"Then take the other one."

"I will," I nodded.

"No, I mean like right now!"

"I'm nervous! What if it's positive?"

"Tann you're gonna be having a baby, and I'm going to be an auntie. Duh! Now, put on your big girl panties, and go take the test!"

"Okay, okay. You're right. Here I go."

I walked into the bathroom and locked the door behind me. After I retrieved the pregnancy test from underneath the sink, I sat on the toilet and stared at it.

"What the fuck are you staring at it for, girl? Pee on that shit! My nerves are on a thousand right now!"

I propped the phone up on the sink, pulled my panties down, and took the test. The next three minutes felt like three years.

"Well, what does it say?" she asked.

I stood up and looked at the stick. I saw one strong pink line and what I thought could have been another line, but I wasn't sure.

"I don't know."

"Bitch, it's not rocket science! Turn the camera around and let me see. I'll tell you!"

I turned the camera around and held it over the test.

"I wish you would keep your hand still so I could see!"

"I'm sorry! I'm nervous. But what does it say? Am I pregnant?" I asked.

"Yeah, Raquel. You're definitely pregnant! Oh my God!" she screamed into the phone. "Congratulations!"

"Thank you." I nodded slowly.

"What's going through your head right now? Are you happy about it?"

"I am... I think. I'm just a little overwhelmed right now. We've talked about trying, but I just didn't think it would happen this fast."

I tried to put how I was feeling into words that Camille would understand, but I just didn't know what to feel. I was numb but excited at the same time. It was just a surreal moment.

"That's understandable. Are you going to tell Law?" she asked, pulling me out of my thoughts.

"I have to."

"So, when are you going to do it? Tonight? Or after you go to the doctor and confirm?"

"Tonight." I nodded.

"Okay, girl. Well, good luck! I'm excited!" She beamed.

"Wish me luck."

Although I still couldn't explain the emotions that were going through my head at the time, the more I talked to Camille, the more excited I started to get. I flashed her a smile and a quick thumbs up then ended the call.

I walked downstairs and searched the bottom level of the house for Law until I ran into him about to walk up the stairs.

"Law," I called his name.

He turned around and looked at me.

"What's up?"

"What are you doing?"

"I was about to come find you to ask if you wanted to go grab some dinner in about an hour or so."

"I was just looking for you, too." I smiled. "Yeah, dinner sounds good, but uh, can you come here really quick?"

Law turned around and walked down the steps to meet me.

"Baby, there's something I have to tell you."

* * *

Law

"Good news or bad news?"

"Good news... I think."

I looked into her eyes and smiled.

"You think? What? You wanna go half on a baby or some-thing?" I joked.

"Maybe." She shrugged.

"What do you mean *maybe*? You don't wanna have my seed no more, Raquel?"

"I didn't say all that."

"Then what are you saying?"

"I'm saying that you're going to be a father."

"Don't play with me."

"I'm not playing." She giggled.

"Are you fuckin' serious, Raquel?"

"I'm serious, Law. I'm pregnant. The test is in the bathroom."

My eyes widened as a wide smile made its way across my face. I jumped up and scooped Raquel into my arms and spun her around.

"Are you happy?" she asked.

"Happy? I'm more than happy, baby!" I smiled as I kissed her lips.

"I can't wait to spend the rest of my life with you, Andreas Calloway."

"Me either, baby."

"So, I guess this means that we need to postpone the wedding until after I deliver?"

"What? Hell no. I want you to have the same last name as my child before we bring him or her into this world, so the show must go on. You gon' wobble your beautiful ass down the aisle to me."

"I love you." She smiled.

"I love you, too."

CHAPTER SEVENTEEN
Blaze

Six Months Later

By the time my brother's wedding day rolled around, Angel was almost eight months old, and I could say that with the help of Raquel, Law, and my mother, I had really started getting the hang of the single parent shit. My daughter had become my best friend. She was turning more and more into her own person with her own personality every day. I was thankful for the opportunity to watch her grow up and to be in a position where I could take care of her.

Although the relationship between my mother and I still wasn't in a good place, I allowed her to see her granddaughter anytime she wanted to. She had been in a better space since she started taking her treatments, but we all knew it would only be a matter of time before she left us, and I didn't want to have that shit on my heart when the day came. As far as any women in my life, there were none. I spent so much time making sure my daughter was straight that I didn't have the time or the patience to entertain another female.

When I pulled up to the church, I saw a face I hadn't seen in months—Camille. I wasn't going to lie; she looked good as hell. The months away from Miami had really made me take a second look at her. I knew we hadn't left off on a good note, but I decided to shoot my shot and at least see if she would accept my apology. I reached in the backseat to get Angel out of the car seat then I walked up to her.

"Excuse me, miss," I said as I gently tapped her on the shoulder.

She turned around and almost looked straight through me.

"Blaze... hey."

"How have you been?"

"I've been well, and yourself?" she asked.

"You know... just hangin' in there, taking life day by day and shit, and just raising my number one girl."

Camille smiled, which made Angel smile back at her.

"Hi, cutie." She smiled.

Angel started jumping in my arms and leaned into Camille while stretching her arms out.

"Oh shit." I chuckled. "She never does that. She must like you."

Camille stretched out her arms and took Angel from me. Angel grabbed her face and started talking baby talk to her while I watched.

"Hey. Um... I just wanted to apologize to you. I was going through a lot of bullshit back then, and I shouldn't have treated you like that or said what I said to you."

"Yeah. Raquel kinda kept me posted about things that went on in your life, and I do wanna say that I'm sorry for your loss. I know this is a big adjustment for you."

"Yeah... it uh... it definitely has been, but we're making it."

"Well, I'm going to give this pretty lady back to you, and I'll see you inside," she said as she turned to walk away.

"Hey, Camille."

"Yeah?"

"Maybe if you find it in your heart to forgive me, we could really try getting to know each other."

"Oh, wow."

"That is if you're interested. No pressure."

"I'm sorry, Blaze, but I'm in a relationship."

"Oh, damn. My fault. I didn't mean no disrespect. I hope you're happy."

"Thank you." She smiled.

"Well, yeah. I guess I'll see you inside."

"Blaze, I was kidding about the relationship shit." She chuckled. "And for the record, I was never *not* interested."

"Oh, word?" I smiled.

"Yeah. *Word*, Blaze."

"Please, call me Aston. I'm tryin' this whole government name shit." I chuckled.

"Aston, huh? I like it."

* * *

Ian

I stared at my reflection in the mirror as I adjusted my shirt collar. The day had finally come for Raquel and me to join as one as husband and wife. It had been a long time coming, but it was worth the wait.

"Are you ready for your big day?" my mother asked as she walked up behind me.

I turned to face her and smiled.

"I am." I nodded.

"And no interruptions this time, right?"

"None whatsoever."

205

My mother smiled and ran her hand down the side of my face. "I'm so proud of you, Andreas."

"For what?"

"For taking care of this family. You remind me more and more of your father every day. Now, I know you may never truly forgive me for everything I've put you through, but I am glad that you allowed me to share your special day with you. It means more to me than you'll ever know."

"Hey, we've all got demons we need to deal with, Ma. You dealt with yours. So as far as I'm concerned, all that shit is water under the bridge. You always gon' be my mother at the end of the day, and I love you."

My mother wrapped her arms around me, and I kissed the top of her head. Although we both knew things would never go back to being as they were before she revealed her secret to us, there was still respect there on my end, because she was the woman who gave me life. I would always love her for that.

"Well," she said, wiping the corners of her eyes. "We better get out there."

I nodded as my mother locked arms with me. We walked out of the back room, and I escorted her to her seat and took my place at the altar beside the preacher. As soon as the music started, I didn't take my eyes off the opposite end of the aisle. I couldn't wait to see Raquel walking down the aisle to me.

Ever since she'd gotten pregnant, she looked more beautiful to me every day. A part of me was nervous about becoming a husband and a father, but with Raquel by my side, I knew we'd be fine.

Blaze nudged me with his elbow, and I snapped out of my trance just in time to see Raquel walking down the aisle. She looked more beautiful than I'd ever seen her look before. If I wasn't a real nigga, I would've probably shed a tear. As soon as my eyes locked onto hers, she smiled.

* * *

Raquel

It was the day I'd dreamed of. It was the day I would finally become Mrs. Andreas Calloway, and I was doing it while pregnant with our fraternal twins. There was nothing standing in the way of our happily ever after. I couldn't help but smile through the happy tears, and I kept my eyes locked on Law's at the end of the aisle.

As soon as I made it to him, he grabbed both of my hands. A part of me felt a rush of PTSD from the first time we'd been standing at the aisle together, but I quickly brushed those thoughts aside and focused on the man I loved in front of me. The preacher cleared his throat and started the ceremony.

"Dearly beloved, we are gathered here today to join Andreas and Raquel together as one in holy matrimony. We will now proceed with the vows. Raquel, would you like to start?"

I nodded and turned to face Law.

"Law, there's not another man on this Earth that will ever make me feel the way you do. You are my life partner, and I vow from this day forward to never leave your side. I will endure any obstacles that come our way, and I will stand by you on the front lines. I promise to love you unconditionally with every breath in my body. I love you, today, tomorrow, and forevermore."

"Andreas, it's your turn."

Law cleared his throat and looked at me. A smile crept across his face as he looked down at my growing belly. He took one of his hands out of mine and placed it on my stomach.

"Raquel, from the moment I met you, I knew there was something different about you. I may not have seen it at first, but you were the one for me, and I can't put into words how happy I am to have you standing across from me today. You're my everything. I will do anything for you to make sure you're smiling for the rest of your life. Raquel, you accept me... flaws and all. Nothing I have has ever impressed you more than me just being myself. I vow to be a protector to you and our unborn children, and to love you and be faithful to you until death do us part."

Although I remained quiet and listened to him talk, I couldn't stop the tears from falling down the sides of my cheeks. In that moment, everything became real to me. Law and I were seconds away from becoming one being, and I couldn't wait.

"Raquel, do you take Andreas as your lawfully wedded husband?"

"I do." I nodded.

"And Andreas, do you take Raquel to be your lawfully wedded wife?"

"I do," he agreed.

"May I have the rings to exchange, please?" the pastor asked. "Raquel, please slip the band on Andreas's finger."

I slid the gold band with diamonds all around it onto Law's ring finger and smiled.

"Please repeat after me. Andreas, with this ring, I thee wed."

"Andreas, baby, with this ring, I thee wed."

Law smiled at me as he slid the wedding band on my finger and repeated after the preacher.

"These wedding rings symbolize a sign of the unbreakable bond that the two of you will share from this day forward," the preacher said.

We both nodded simultaneously.

"By the power vested in me and the state of Florida, I now pronounce you husband and wife. Ladies and gentlemen, I now present to you Mr. and Mrs. Andreas Calloway. Andreas, you may salute your bride."

When the preacher gave Law the green light to kiss me, he pulled me into his arms and kissed me in a way that he'd never kissed me before. I never wanted it to end.

"I love you so much, baby." I smiled.

Law wiped the corners of my eyes and kissed me again.

"I love you more, Mrs. Calloway."

EPILOGUE
Raquel

Three Months Later

I woke up in the middle of the night to use the bathroom for what felt like the hundredth time. As soon as I flipped on the lights, I felt a pop inside my vagina then water gushed down my legs. I figured since I was on my way to use the bathroom I had just peed on myself a little, but before I could sit down on the toilet, I felt the gush again.

"Oh, shit!" I said as I looked down at the wet floor. "Law! Law! Baby, wake up!"

Law stirred in his sleep and then sat up slowly.

"What's wrong, baby?"

"Law, I think my water just broke."

"Oh shit," he said as he quickly sat up and turned on the light beside the bed.

"It's time, baby."

Law jumped up and ran over to me as I stood in the doorframe between the bedroom and the bathroom.

"Are you sure?"

"Yeah, bring me my phone so I can call the doctor."

"Let's not even waste time. I'm about to take you to the hospital right now."

Since I had lost sight of my feet shortly after our wedding, he helped me slide on a pair of sweatpants and some slippers.

"Yo, Blaze! Blaze! Get in here!" he yelled.

Blaze came running into the room like he was trying to find out where the fire was.

"What? What's going on?"

"Raquel is in labor. Can you start the car? I gotta carry her down the stairs."

"Yeah. Let me just take Angel over to stay with Mom real quick," he said.

"Okay. Thanks."

Law scooped me into his arms and slowly carried me down the steps.

"Don't worry, baby. Everything is going to be okay."

By the time we were halfway to the hospital, my contractions had started to kick in. They were short but not intense, so I could still breathe through them. After I was admitted, I was taken back into the labor and delivery area and hooked up to monitors so the doctor could keep an eye on the babies' heartbeats.

The longer I sat with my back against the bed, the more uncomfortable I got. Law helped me turn over on my right side to ease the pain. It was finally sinking in. I was about to become a mother of two. I dreaded delivery from the moment the stick turned pink. I didn't handle pain well, and I was squeamish when it came to blood, especially my own. By the time the doctor came back in three hours later, my contractions had worsened, but I was ten centimeters dilated and had been given the green light to push.

"Okay, Raquel. I need you to push down and hold for ten seconds, okay? Ready? One, two, push!" the head nurse told me.

I pushed down like she said, and the doctor said he could see the first baby crowning. Law stood by my side and held my leg as I pushed for another ten seconds.

"Ahhhhhhhh!" I screamed.

At 6:43 a.m., Andreas Jr. was born. Two minutes later, Amani, our daughter came into the world. Once she was out, the doctor passed her over to the nurses, and they started cleaning her up beside her brother. The nurses suctioned out their tiny mouths and noses. Their lungs filled with air, letting out the most beautiful cries I'd ever heard. They wrapped them up in pink and blue blankets and laid them across my chest. I gently brushed the back of my fingers against their cheeks and kissed each of their foreheads. They had the softest skin and looked like the perfect mix of Law and me. I was overjoyed as I looked down at the bundles of joy in my arms and smiled bright and wide.

"Welcome to the world, Andreas Jr. and Amani Calloway."

THE END

Afterword

Readers,

Thanks for following along with me on my literary journey so far. Also, thank you for reading the final installment of the *In The Arms of a Savage* series. Got a second to leave a review? If you've made it this far, I hope you'll consider taking a minute to tell me what you thought about the book. I thoroughly enjoy reading them! Why does this matter? I'm always striving to attract new readers and retain current ones, and reviews are one of the easiest ways to attract readers. If you loved the book, tell a friend, and most importantly, let me know!

K.L. Hall

Other books by K.L. Hall:

Diary of a Hood Princess 1-3

Rise of a Street King: The Justice Silva Story *(Spin-Off to the Diary of a Hood Princess series)*

Broken Condoms and Promises 1-3

In the Arms of a Savage 1-3

Built for a Savage: Blaze and Camille's Love Story *(Spin-Off to the In the Arms of a Savage Series)*

A Ruthle$$ Love Story 1-3

Fallin' for the Alpha of the Streets 1-2

The Most Savage of Them All: The Wolfe Calloway Story *(Prequel to the In the Arms of a Savage Series)*

When a Gangsta Loves a Good Girl

Caught Between My Husband and a Hustler

The Illest Taboo 1-2

To the Only Thug I'll Ever Love

A Lover's Heist: Chief and Gianna's Love Story

A Lover's Heist II: Rome and Lira's Love Story

A Lover's Heist III: Baby and Skai's Love Story

Crushed Velvet & Cashmere

Crushed Velvet & Cashmere 2

Entanglements

Never Had a Bad Boy Love Me So Good

Good Girls Always Got a Thing for the Thugs

Professor Zaddy: A Potomac Falls Novel

Bound in the Arms of a Thug: Chop & Kendyl's Love Story

Make Mine a Gangsta: The Patton Brothers Book One

Gimme a Gangsta: The Patton Brothers Book Two

In the Arms of a Savage 1-3

Short Reads + Novellas:

Bi-Curious: An Erotic Tale

Bi-Curious 2: Tastes Like Candy

A Savage Calloway Christmas *(Christmas novella to the In the Arms of a Savage Series)*

Lovin' the Alpha of the Streets: A Valentine's Day Novella *(Valentine's Day novella to the Fallin' for the Alpha of the Streets Series)*

Awakened: A Paranormal Romance

As Long as You Stay Down

Solace in Seven

Solace II: The Final Cut

Something Bleu

Something Borrowed

Something New

The Knight Before Christmas: A Potomac Falls Short

I'll Be Home for Christmas: A Potomac Falls Short Book II

Triggered: A Potomac Falls Novella

Wasted Off You: A Friends to Lovers Novella

Because You Don't Know My Name: A Potomac Falls Novella

Will You Say My Name: A Potomac Falls Novella Book Two

Remember My Name: A Potomac Falls Novella Book Three

Every Thug Needs a Lady: A Lady and the Tramp Retelling

Ten Things I Hate About Lovin' You: An Enemies to Lovers Novella

In Exchange: An Urban Thriller

T.A.N.: An Erotic Novella

<u>A Gangsta's Love Language: A Patton Brothers Spin-Off</u>

Children's Books:

Princess for Hire

Princess Twinkle Toes & the Missing Magic Sneakers

Little One, Change the World

Adjust Your Crown: A Self-Love Coloring Book for Children of Color

Non-Fiction:

Authors are a Business: The Booked & Busy Course Mini Book

Sign up for my mailing list to stay updated with new releases, giveaways, sneak peeks, and more! Click this link: https://bit.ly/38RMpV5

Connect with me on social media:

Facebook: https://www.facebook.com/authorklhall

Twitter: https://twitter.com/authorklhall

Instagram: https://www.instagram.com/officialklhall/

Website: https://www.authorklhall.com.

Printed in France by Amazon
Brétigny-sur-Orge, FR

29600768R00132